DEDICATED TO CLEVELAND.

THE CLEVELAND COFFEE KILLER

A MISTY CHEEVIS MYSTERY

—

BY **KELLEN ALEXANDER**

FRONT COVER PAINTING BY **JEAN SEESTADT**

DESIGN, LAYOUT, & BACK ILLUSTRATION BY **BRIAN BARR**

© 2021

PROLOGUE

-

Well, it's the last page of my journal. My therapist Janice says I should look back and reflect upon where I've come since I first opened this thing and wrote the words: FUCK THIS SHIT.

I admit, I've come a long way since I first started writing--after Janice forced me to try journaling. She thought I might like it on account of how I have a "way with words" as she put it. The dumb cunt.

But hey, I'm already finished with my first journal, so who's the dumb cunt after all? Probably me. But I've always known that. That's what landed me in therapy in the first place.

Court ordered therapy for stalking Dean, my manager at Pizza Fever. Allegedly! But also legally proven in court, I guess, according to my court-ordered therapist Janice. She said I should stop saying "allegedly" because I was literally convicted in a court of law.

But I still don't think I did anything wrong. I found out and had PROOF that Dean, my manager, was embezzling from Pizza Fever. But no thanks there. He's apparently "engaged" to Becky and her parents own the stupid pizza company so they swept it under the rug like they do all the dropped pepperoni BY THE WAY. Disgusting.

One month later they fired my dumb ass for not paying for my Mountain Dew and then slapped charges and a restraining order on me because they have video of me tailing Dean's Ford Fiesta for 12 miles. Not my fault he drove around like an idiot for 12 miles! He coulda stopped sooner! Gas is $2.73 a gallon, jackass.

Anyways, the therapy was for stalking Dean. The jail time was for assaulting him in an Aldi. I knew I shoulda waited and jumped him on his way out, but sometimes I just can't contain myself. I know that about myself. I'm like a velociraptor or another top-tier predator. I don't just bite back. I bite first and you'll never see me coming. You might hear me though because I pop champagne and I'm dripping in ice. Clank clank. New money. Solid gold. 36 carrots. And 3 bags of kale, as it turns out. Aldi has organic food and I buy that. Well, I was forced to pay for it after I whacked Dean in the face with the carrots and the kale. I didn't come here to make friends. I came here for Mama Cozzi's Pizza Kitchen Frozen Pizza Bites and a 2-liter of Coke but UNFORTUNATELY I had to run into my stupid corrupt ex-boss before I got to checkout. I could just tell in his eyes that he was itching for a beating. So I complied. And that's how I ended up in jail. Never even got my frozen pizza bites.

Where was I? Oh yeah. The beginning of this journal. Things were bad. I spent 60 days in jail. I had to write in a gay ass journal every day. But I'm getting out of here now and I can be done with therapy and I can get on with my bitchass life.

Well looks like I'm reaching the last few lines of this stupid thing. Janice says I should save these journals, but I want to burn mine. For security reasons and because I like fire.

Much love to everyone may the Lord bless and keep you in his holy name except may Pizza Fever burn to the ground and may the rain wash its ashes down the drain with my stinky doo doo.

Amen.

— Misty Cheevis

CHAPTER ONE

-

NOT MUCH CHANGES IN CLEVELAND over 60 days--or ever for that matter--but the weather in mid-October was certainly different than the weather in mid-July, leaving Misty stuck standing in the rain at the bus stop outside the Cuyahoga County Department of Corrections in the same clothing she went in with: an XXL Tweety-Bird t-shirt, plaid pajama pants and men's slippers.

Misty was dripping wet when the bus finally pulled up.

"You look wet," the bus driver noticed as Misty swiped her pass in the machine.

"No shit, Sherlock," Misty bursted out forcefully before sloshing to the back of the bus.

"If he weren't a city employee I so would have threatened his ass," Misty thought to herself as she found her way to her seat. "I would have threatened him hard."

Today was not the day to mess with Misty. She'd just gotten out of jail. Or maybe it was the day to mess with her: she was on parole and wouldn't be able to retaliate.

She was hungry and horny. The food in jail was shit and all the people there were prudes. She didn't get any protein and she didn't get any ass. Right now all she could think about was getting to her boyfriend's apartment. She was hoping he'd grown some balls while she was gone and he'd finally be willing to tie her up or spit on her or something.

"Yeesh," she said. "I got the window all fogged up."

She rubbed the bottom of her shirt on the foggy window and looked out over the industrial valley as the bus rumbled past. The eternal flame of the multinationally-owned steel mill's smokestack could be seen through the mist.

"Smells like eggs," Misty thought to herself. "They making steel in there or they making breakfast? What the fuck?" She pulled her t-shirt over her nose. The shirt had a cartoon of an angry Tweety Bird on it with text reading: I have three sides. The sweet side. The fun and crazy side. And the side you never want to see.

Misty hopped off the bus directly into a puddle. Her slippers were already soaked so it wasn't that big of a deal, but Misty flipped off the bus driver with both her middle fingers anyway as he pulled away.

"Dick."

Misty wiped her wet, sandy-blonde hair out of her face and sloshed her way down a sleepy side street. Hundred-year-old multi-family homes sat closely beside each other, each one displaying a different approach to degradation. Some leaned into it, with trash on the front porch and "BEWARE OF DOG" signs hanging crookedly from rusty wire fencing. Others did their best to evoke a little charm amidst the circumstances, sprinkling in some landscaping and a Puerto Rican flag hanging by the stoop. Others displayed the delicate care of an elderly person who'd ushered the neighborhood through brighter days, while some bared the charm of a flowering overgrown shrub, thriving from being left alone.

Misty approached a dirty-white duplex with a wild patch of yard. She was relieved to be standing under the roof of the front porch, which was missing some pegs in the railing. She hit the buzzer. There was no answer. After hitting it a few more times she went out into the rain to look up at the second floor window. A light was on upstairs and she knew Dustin rarely left the house. After a second, the curtain moved and the light went out.

"Dumbass," Misty said to herself before leaping up the front steps to lay her elbow on the buzzer. After a minute and a half of buzzing, the door finally unlocked and Misty let herself in.

"What the fuck, douchebag!?" Misty hollered as she pounded her way up, her slippers leaving wet footprints on the dusty, creaking stairs.

"Oh, hi Misty," Dustin said, standing in the doorway to the apartment. "I didn't know you were getting out today."

"Yeah, I was gonna tell you my release date when you paid me a visit, sweetheart, but seems like maybe you lost the address to the jail or something since I never saw you there," she said sarcastically as she shoved her way past Dustin into the sparsely decorated apartment. She went directly to the bedroom and started rifling through the dresser drawers. "Where's my stuff? I need to change."

She came back into the living room where Dustin was seated in his usual spot on the grungy plaid couch, where he'd spent endless hours playing X-Box. "I thought I left some jean shorts here? I need some dry clothes."

"You wanna borrow some jeans? Most of mine aren't too dirty." Dustin was wearing a tight crew neck sweatshirt and a pair of khakis. On his feet were a pair of nice, fresh, all black Air Jordans.

"Nice kicks," Misty mentioned before she took off her wet shirt and pajama pants and started rifling through the pile of clothes left on Dustin's bed. She took a big sniff of a pair of men's boxers and gagged. "So what did you do while I was gone? You working?"

"A little. I'm waiting for it to start snowing and then I'm gonna plow."

"Cool," Misty said as she sniffed another pair, shrugged and pulled them on. Still topless, her large, pale, pink breasts hanging free, her nipples hard with the chill, she perused the kitchen. She returned munching on a Slim-Jim. "You wanna fuck or what?"

"Huh? Uh…" Dustin squirmed on the couch.

"Huh? Uh?" Misty mimicked. "What's wrong with you, bro? Why are you acting so weird?"

"Weird? I'm not being weird."

"Yes you are. Why aren't you playing X-Box right now? And where did you get these boxers? These are Old Navy. These new?"

"No they're not."

"Yes they are. And so are those shoes. And there's Slim-Jim's and Gatorade in the kitchen. And you don't have a job. What's up, bro? Since when do you grocery shop?"

Dustin just stared at the ground.

"You gonna make me say it?" Misty asked.

Dustin gulped.

Misty grabbed all the clothes from off Dustin's bed and started hurling them at him. "Who! Is! SHE!? Do I know the bitch?" She emphasized the words with each thrown item of clothing, "Who...is...this...WHORE!"

"She's not a whore! She goes to church with my mom! You don't know her!"

"An older woman!? That explains the Slim Jim's and Gatorade. Can't take care of yourself you dumb slob! Where's my stuff! I want my jean shorts, my t-shirts, everything! Get it or I SUE your ass."

Dustin scurried into his room. He looked through his drawers and closet, shoving aside empty gatorade bottles and bags of cold french fries. Eventually, he pulled a plastic grocery bag out from underneath his bed. Inside were Misty's jean shorts and some t-shirts: Bugs Bunny, Myrtle Beach and a blue Best Buy Polo. Misty pulled on a dry crew neck that said "Harvard" on it. She tried to pull on the jean shorts but they were too small. "Damn it."

"She get you those Jordan's too? Old Navy and Jordans? Geez, is your mom friends with the Queen of England? You piece of shit!"

"No! Linda said I needed to grow up. She told me to get some church shoes, so I bought the Jordans. I paid for them myself, though, for your information."

Misty laughed.

"Oh, right. With what money?" She was busy looking under the couch and underneath the random shit that was left lying around the living room, grabbing more of her stuff to shove into her plastic grocery bag. "Where the hell is my X-Box?"

Dustin looked at Misty with pathetic, guilty eyes.

"Our X-box," Dustin replied. His voice cracking. "We split it..."

"Yeah, so? Where is it?"

Dustin looked down at the floor, his fancy new Air Jordans a tracing a figure eight on the floor.

"You sold my X-Box? For shoes?!" Misty yelled. "Fuck you!"

"Our X-Box. I'm in a serious relationship, now, Misty. I don't have time for video games. I have church and church choir to keep me busy. Anyways it's better for you not to have the X-Box. I think first person shooters really aggravate your rage issues."

"RAGE ISSUES!?"

Misty's face turned a bright red and her eyes bulged out.

Dustin limped to a stop as the #6 bus pulled away. "Misty! Get back here! My shoe!"

Misty shoved one black Air Jordan into her blue grocery bag and dropped into a seat at the back of the bus.

"Our shoes, jackass."

Dustin stood with one shoe and one wet sock as the bus pulled away.

CHAPTER TWO

−

Now that it was the middle of October, the sun was setting earlier. It was just before dusk and the sky was glowing a dark blue as Misty arrived at her Grandmother's home: a narrow little ranch with pale green vinyl siding and white shutters. Another neighborhood from a time long gone, Grammy's 1930's bungalow was one of the only remaining homes from a time of hopeful development. Now, it sat amongst empty lots, expensive minimalist condos and prefab industrial homes.

Misty was exhausted and spent the entire bus-ride fantasizing about her air-mattress.

"I'm home! Grammy, where you at? Misty's outta jail baby, let's go! Can we get Chick-Fil-A tonight?" Misty hurled her grocery bag of possessions where it would normally land on the couch. Instead, it slammed against a barren wall and fell to the ground. Misty looked around the living room. There were a bunch of boxes and all of her grandma's stupid knick-knacks were missing from the shelves.

Grammy walked down the hall, out of the kitchen. She was wearing a grey velour sweatsuit, gold hoop earrings, frosty pink lip gloss and pink Nike Air Force 1's. Her hair was gelled, spiked and dyed platinum blonde.

"Misty! Oh, honey. You're home. Come here, biscuit."

She pulled Misty into a formal presentation of a hug, her manicured nails hovering an inch underneath Misty's elbows as she placed her face beside Misty's making kissing sounds, but never making contact.

"You look good!" she said, with a bright smile as Misty stood, blinking, in sopping wet men's flannel boxers.

"Jail fucking sucks. What in the bejeezus is going on in here? Exterminators come again? We still have bedbugs? But we got rid of the beds!"

Grammy looked at the boxes and let out a sigh. "Oh, Misty. Maybe you should sit down."

"Sit down where? Where's the couch? Those little fuckers got in the couch, too? Hell!"

"No, Misty. There were no bedbugs. Honey, I... I have something to tell you. It happened kind of sudden and I didn't know how to tell you and it's actually kind of exciting for me--thrilling really--"

Grammy pulled out her lip gloss and applied another layer.

"Well, what in the heck?"

"Misty, dear. I'm engaged to Mr. Chip Jizzlin and we're moving to Florida." She pronounced the word "Florida" like "Flarda." We're moving to Flarda.

"What? Who's Chip Jizzlin?"

Grammy paced the room, sorting her things with a nervous smile.

"Mr. Chip is the fellow I met at Bingo a few months ago? Remember?"

"Wait--is this the creep who pulled me aside at church during the passing of the peace to tell me he convinced you to get a prescription for vagina cream?"

"Yes, Imvexxy. It treats vulvar and vaginal dryness caused by menopause. He only told you so that you would keep an eye out for me as there can sometimes be side effects from the medication, like hives or diarrhea. He just wanted you to look out for me when he couldn't be around. He's so sweet."

"I can't believe you let some fool convince you to get on dangerous medication just so he can raw dog you without lube. I'm gonna vomit."

"It's not a dangerous medication, Misty. It helps a lot of mature women. You don't have anything to worry about. The only side effects we've noticed so far have been the enlarged breasts and rapid growth in pubic hair--both of which pleases Mr. Chip very much."

"You're marrying that creep?"

Grammy continued packing away her things into boxes and plastic bins.

"Yes and we're moving to Flarda. I actually have to be out of here tomorrow. It's quite sudden but the house sold really fast! Apparently this is an up-and-coming area! Who knew?"

"Tomorrow! Grammy! What the hell?"

"Got a great price for it, too! Bought myself some fancy sneakers. Cute, huh?"

Grammy showed off her pink Air Force 1's to Misty.

"Hello? Where am I supposed to live?"

"I thought you were still gonna be in jail. I sent you a letter so you'd know. I'm sorry, honey. But you know I've always wanted to move to Flarda. And Mr. Chip promised me we'd do it in a hot tub, which is a dream I've had ever since I stayed up late and I caught that film "Wild Things" playing on TNT. Whew! Two busty ladies and a guy in a pool. Hot stuff."

Misty maneuvered herself through the boxes to get closer to Grammy. She waved her hand in front of Grammy's face to hopefully get her attention.

"Hello? Those are both my dreams! I wanted to move to Flarda! And I DVR'd that movie! That's MY dream! And you're just leaving me homeless!"

"You can go stay with that fellow you were seeing. The one who can't grow facial hair."

"No! I actually can't! He's dating a Sunday School teacher!"

Grammy looked up from her task with pride.

"Well, good for him!"

Misty backed into the barren wall and slid down it until she was seated on the floor with her hands around her knees.

"I can't believe this. I'm being abandoned by the only family I know. Just because she's a slave to the penis. Good God, woman! You're old. Have some dignity. Didn't you fight for the right to vote and shit?"

Grammy came and sat down next to Misty. She put her arm around Misty, gently.

"You know, Misty, this might actually be good for you. You can't always rely on your Grammy to take care of you. In fact, this is just what you need. You had a good job making pizzas and you threw it all away because of your childish behavior. It's about time you move in with a man. Learn to take care of yourself. Build a home. Learn to cook. And you might want to learn to stop cussing for one thing. It's not cute. Is that why that chubby little man left you? You know with an attitude like yours you're gonna get yourself in even more trouble than you've already been in. And if you wind up dead I don't want to be watching from behind the gates of heaven as you are denied entry because of your shenanigans. Do you know how hard that would be for me and Chip?"

Misty stared at her Grandma, shocked and angry. Her grandma wasn't wrong. Misty didn't want to keep getting into trouble. And it was time for her to grow up. Misty wanted to grow up! But was it really necessary to kick her out onto the street and condemn her to an eternity in hell?

"Well you can stay here tonight, Misty." Grammy stood up and did a few stretches. "You'll have the whole place to yourself. Mr. Chip Jizzlin is picking me up and I'll be spending the night at his two-bedroom two-bath in West Park. Did I tell you he has a fancy new sleep number mattress from Dick Vagantis Cleveland Mattress?"

Misty had been watching commercials for the local Cleveland mattress company on TV and seeing his billboards lining the highway since she was a kid. All while spending her nights on an air mattress. She scowled.

"I put the phone number on the refrigerator in case you need anything," Grammy said, as she made her way to the kitchen in the back of the house.

"I thought you don't want me asking you for anything anymore," Misty called to the back of the house, sarcastically.

"Misty. Stop being such an ass," Grammy responded. "I'll just be in Flarda if you need me. And, listen. The Corolla isn't gonna make it down there. So, I decided to give it to you. The title is in an envelope on the fridge."

Misty joined her grandma in the kitchen.

"Title? You giving me a car or a book? Don't play games with me right now! I'm tired!"

"I'm giving you the car, Misty. Please take care of it, honey."

A horn honked twice outside.

"All right, Mr. Chip is here. He has a romantic evening planned for us."

She looked through her purse and pulled out a small tube.

"Aha! Can't forget my Imvexxy! Love you, peanut!"

Grammy smooched Misty and pranced out the front door.

Misty stood on the front stoop, her arms folded and scowling as Grammy and Mr. Chip Jizzlin pulled away, laughing out loud in his red Mazda Miata.

CHAPTER THREE

-

MISTY COULD HAVE STAYED at her grandma's house all day feeling sorry for herself, but Misty wasn't the type to sit and sulk. And on top of that, there was nowhere to sit, since all of Grammy's furniture was packed up for her stupid move.

Misty wasn't afraid of work. In fact, she liked work. She liked it so much that when she saw someone stealing from her workplace, she put in extra hours investigating the crime! Off the clock for that matter!

Janice had told her to stop dwelling on the past. That it wasn't healthy to keep replaying the events in her head, no matter how unjust they were. Janice said to focus on something positive. Misty put Janice's words to practice and decided to spend her day finding a job. She would need some income if she was going to be renting an apartment or whatever.

Misty sauntered into the public library, chewing on a Slim-Jim she'd stolen from Dustin.

"Excuse me, you can't have food in here," the librarian noted from the desk.

Misty stuffed the entire beef jerky into her mouth. She held up the greasy wrapper. "You got a twash can?" she asked, crumbles of spiced meat flying out of her mouth.

The librarian, a skinny man with blue-light-cancelling glasses and long, scraggly hair, pointed to a nearby bin. Misty threw the item out and then leaned on the library counter. She gulped down the last bits of jerky.

"So you got computers here or what?" she asked, without even looking around the facility.

The librarian pointed to the row of computers just behind Misty.

"They free?"

"Yes, ma'am."

"I can apply for jobs on there?"

"Sure. You can submit online applications."

"Is there a website for that?"

The librarian let out a frustrated sigh. He was hoping this lady would just go away so he could get on with his business, but she just kept asking questions. He determined that the best way to get her away from him was, sadly, to actually help her.

"You know, there is a site that lets you apply for a whole set of retail jobs in the area, you just have to fill out a preliminary questionnaire and then you're eligible to apply for a whole bunch of jobs in the area with the click of a button."

"What jobs?"

"Large corporations mostly. I think Dillards is part of the program. TJ Maxx, Marshalls, Wendy's, Home Depot... you know. The kinds of stores you'd find in a shopping plaza."

"Plaza? Sounds fancy. Let's do it."

The librarian helped Misty find the service online.

"Here we go, so it starts with personal information. Address?"

"Address?" Misty cringed. She entered her grandma's address, knowing full well it wouldn't be her address after tomorrow.

"All right. The rest of it is the questionnaire. Just fill this out and it will send your application off to all the different corporations. I'll leave you to finish the questionnaire," the librarian said softly as he cautiously backed away, like one would after placing a precarious block in a high-stakes game of jenga.

The survey asked participants to rank how much they agree or disagree with a variety of statements, including:

My goals in life are clear.

Misty could choose strongly disagree, disagree, neutral, agree or strongly agree.

"My goals in life are clear..." Misty thought to herself. "Yeah, my goal is get a job and a place to live. Strongly agree."

If people are rude to me, I just shrug it off.

"Strongly disagree. Don't mess with me. Better if they know that. Click."

I prefer working in a stable, rather than flexible environment.

"Stable? That'd be a cool job. I love horses." Strongly Agree.

I am ambitious.

"Nope. I can only write with my right hand. Strongly Disagree, bitch."

You swear when you argue.

Misty looked around the library and then discreetly clicked Strongly Disagree.

The survey questions continued on and on.

You like to be in the middle of a large crowd. Neutral.

You like to plan things before you do them. Neutral.

You hate to give up if you can't solve a hard problem. Neutral, Neutral, Neutral, Neutral.

Misty sat with her head resting in her hand. She was getting bored with the questionnaire and completed the page by just clicking Neutral for every question.

After what seemed like forever, Misty reached the final question.

Have you ever been convicted of a crime? Yes or No.

Misty scowled and clicked "Yes."

Immediately the screen turned red and bold letters stated: You are not eligible for the common application. Please submit applications on paper at individual locations. Thank you.

The rest of the library disappeared and Misty stared at the red screen through tunnel vision. She could feel her blood boiling up. Her ears started ringing and she felt like she was under water. She started breathing heavy and loud like a wild boar.

"Fuck!" Misty screamed. She slammed her hands on the computer keyboard and stood up from her seat at the computer station. She clenched her fist and stood up. She turned to the nearby bookshelf and punched the first thing she saw: a child's shoebox diorama. The art project flung off the shelf and slammed against a window behind it, frightening a woman walking by.

"Security!" yelled the long-haired librarian, fumbling with the old telephone on his desk. An 8-year-old girl cried over her destroyed art project.

"I'm leaving! I'm leaving! Geez!" Misty hurried out of the library, in a cold sweat.

Misty's heart raced as she quickly fled the scene.

"I'm going to have to be more careful," Misty though to herself. The last thing she needed was to get into more trouble with the law. She was on probation. One wrong step and she could end up back in jail.

Misty continued toward the main drag of her grandma's neighborhood. It had been a rough first day of freedom. Her boyfriend dumped her, her grammy left town, she destroyed an innocent child's art project and to top it all off, she was homeless.

And so her air mattress wasn't the only thing that felt deflated as Misty walked down the street looking for a place that might hire someone with a totally understandable, extremely justified criminal history. Literally anyone in Misty's men's slippers would have assaulted that loser in the Aldi. Why this should preclude Misty from EMPLOYMENT went far beyond Misty's sense of justice. Someone like Misty couldn't comprehend the morality of the modern age. To her, it was as complicated as calculus or baseball statistics.

Misty looked up and down the street of her grandma's "up and coming" neighborhood. It wasn't anything special, but construction had begun on some swanky new condos called "The Breach."

Other than that were a few mom and pop type shops scattered up and down the street, interspersed with vacant storefronts. A large national chain in a fancy shopping plaza might disqualify Misty based on her history, but perhaps it was less likely for a local small business to instantly seek information into Misty's criminal past. Certainly one of these establishments could use the help of a hardworking, passionate young woman who is willing to work on saying fewer swears in casual conversation.

She popped into a hair salon. An elderly woman sat under a hair dryer reading a copy of Cleveland Dogs magazine. In another chair a woman was having her hair washed in the sink by a stylist in a black apron.

"You guys hiring?"

"We could maybe use a part-time receptionist."

"You do background checks?" Misty asked.

The hair stylist was a little thrown off.

"Background checks? Um… yeah, is that gonna be a problem?"

Misty stood in the doorway thinking this over. She silently left the salon and proceeded down the street.

"Okay," Misty thought to herself. "That was stupid. I shouldn't bring up the background checks."

Misty came upon a tattoo parlor.

"Aha," she thought as she stepped inside. "A tattoo parlor. These motherfuckers can't be afraid of a criminal background."

A large man with a beard sat at his station, drawing designs on paper. "Can I help you?"

"You hiring?"

"For what?"

"Anything, I need work."

"What can you do?"

"Whatever you need! I'm asking you!" Misty was wondering what was so hard about the question: you need help or no? Jesus Christ!

"Can you tattoo?"

"Probably. I got a tattoo of a slutty butterfly above my ass, didn't seem that hard. You wanna see it?"

Misty turned around and pulled her shirt up a little bit and her pants down a little to reveal the tattoo and a little peek of ass crack. It was pretty sweet and slutty.

"That's a sweet tattoo. But, listen, if you don't have experience, I don't think we have anything for you."

"Come on. Let me try at least. I can learn quick."

"Fine. Why don't you draw something and show me what you can do?"

Misty saddled up at the desk and grabbed a pencil. "All right. What do you want me to draw?"

"How about your dream tattoo."

"All right, all right. I can do that. Give me some space, bro." Misty pushed the artist away and began carefully drawing.

She took her time. She focused hard, carefully drawing and occasionally furiously erasing things. She drew with her face close to her page, close enough that her hot breath moistened the paper. She hovered over her work, periodically looking over her shoulder at the tattoo artist as if he was trying to cheat off her in a high school exam.

Finally she was done. "Done!"

The tattoo artist came over and looked at her picture. On the soft, crumpled paper, behind the smudged graphite and beneath the eraser shavings, was a juvenile, poorly drawn dragon that looked like it was done by a 4-year-old. The dragon was emerging from behind what appeared to be a pair of fuzzy dice. Text read "R.I.P. Steve Irwin <3"

"How about that?" Misty said proudly. "Dream tattoo."

"That's... nice. You know, I think we're going to look for someone else, but thanks for stopping in." He showed her to the door.

"Well then you can suck my dick because this place smells like Cool Ranch Doritos anyway!"

Misty stormed out of the tattoo parlor. After a few steps, she turned around and went back in.

"Can I keep that drawing?"

Misty had some trouble with the people at the computer repair place. They asked if she could repair a hard drive and she shoved a screwdriver in the disc drive and couldn't get it out. At the antique store she knocked over $250 worth of pyrex cookware while demonstrating that she'd have no problem chasing and tackling shoplifters. When the owner of the comic book store asked Misty if she had a favorite comic, Misty said, "Seinfeld."

It was looking grim as Misty made enemies with every establishment on the main street of her grandma's neighborhood. Misty felt herself getting angry. She employed the breathing techniques suggested to her by her court-ordered therapist Janice. She sounded like a steam-powered train, but she eventually calmed herself down.

She couldn't afford to cause any trouble, not now. The absolute last thing she needed was trouble with the law. She was growing tired and her stomach was growling as she stopped into "Coffee Bucket," a small shop emitting a warm glow.

Inside, dim lights illuminated rustic wooden floors and exposed brick walls. Lush and lively houseplants adorned shelves and tables, scattered amongst a few cozy chairs and couches.

The only person inside was the barista, who was clearly cleaning and shutting down the shop for the evening. Misty plopped down on a stool at the counter. The barista was removing pastries from the pastry case and tossing them in the trash.

"Whoa! You just gonna throw those out?" Misty wailed.

"We close in five minutes," she warned Misty. "So if you want coffee, you're gonna have to take it to go."

"Fine! I don't even like coffee. You got hot chocolate?"

The barista didn't even respond. She opened the fridge, slammed a bottle of chocolate milk on the counter, slammed a pitcher on the counter and bitterly steamed up a hot chocolate for Misty. The barista had dark hair, pulled up into a messy bun. She wore a striped yellow and red t-shirt tucked into high-waisted pleated slacks. She didn't wear any makeup, but had on round, wire rimmed glasses and geometric, ceramic red earrings. Her skin was whiter than Misty's, which was shocking since Misty had spent the last month indoors.

Misty admired the tattoos that adorned the barista's arm as she shoved the paper cup of hot chocolate in front of her. "$3.50."

"$3.50 for a hot chocolate!" Misty recoiled. "Shit! Can I change my mind?"

"No. Pay up or get out."

Misty could tell the barista wasn't messing around.

"Shit." Misty counted out the change in her pocket and slid it across the counter. "So you guys hiring?" she asked as the barista counted out the change.

The barista stopped what she was doing and looked at Misty. Her eyes narrowed, suspiciously.

"Do you have a resume?"

"If you got a piece of paper, I got a resume. Been cutting lawns since I was 6. Landscaping, really. Used to cut my ex-boyfriend's hair and his friend's hair. It may sound like I'm mostly in the cutting business but I can grow stuff too. I'm growing skills by the day. Growing my bag. You know the drill."

"Any coffee experience?"

"I've had the stuff. I once broke a Keurig at the Urgent Care. But I put it back together and that should tell you something."

The barista closed her eyes and took a deep breath.

"A lot of people think being a barista is easy work but it isn't, you know. And we're an up and coming shop here in Cleveland. We roast our own beans and so our customers expect knowledgeable and skilled baristas. We take pride in our coffee and in our service."

Misty rolled her eyes. This coffee lady had a big head and Misty wanted to poke a pin in it.

"It tastes okay, but I wouldn't get my panties in a clump over it."

"You're not even drinking the coffee. You know, save your resume. I don't think it would be a good fit. Maybe you'd be better off at a Speedway or something."

The barista continued to gather up used dishes, tossing them into a plastic bin.

"They hiring?"

"We're closing in 5 minutes," the barista called out as she dropped the dishes in soapy water.

"Great, I'm enjoying myself. I think I'll stay for another five. Might grab one of those muffins out of the trash there, don't think it looks too contaminated..."

Misty leaned over the counter and peered down into the trash can. The barista quickly grabbed the bag and began to tie it up.

"I'm actually taking the trash out, if you don't mind."

The barista took out a key, stared at Misty and then locked the cash register before she walked into the back room and then through a door to the alley outside, leaving both doors open.

"God, this place sucks ass too," Misty thought to herself. "Who'd even want to work here. Boring."

Misty sat there waiting for the barista to return and kick her out, but the barista didn't come back. Misty looked at the clock. It was an old-school clock with a minute hand and hour hand and stuff so it took Misty some effort to figure out what time it was. She stared at the clock.

"It's either 7:15 or 3:45... shit. I thought she wanted to close at 7 o'clock." Misty sat there awkwardly. She wanted to prove a point that she wasn't going to leave and maybe provoke a fight, but this was just getting boring.

Eventually, Misty got up and pushed open the door into the back room. She could see that the back room was empty and the rear exit was still open and the cool autumn air was blowing in from the dark alley behind the shop.

Misty crept through the back. "Hey, lady! You out there? Hot chocolate's cold. I think I need warm-up."

A couple of used paper coffee cups with the name "Coffee Bucket" blew past in the wind, along with some napkins. They drifted past one of the old muffins from the pastry case.

"Aha!" Misty said, creeping toward the muffin on the asphalt. "Still good!" she called out.

But as she reached down to grab the muffin, she noticed a dense trail of trash: cups, napkins and half-eaten pastries. Her eyes followed the trail to the dumpster.

"Oh, FUCK!"

Just past the ripped open trash bag, laying on the asphalt next to the dumpster, was the angry barista in a puddle of blood, her neck sliced deep from ear to ear. A box cutter lay on the asphalt, dripping with blood.

"Shit!"

Misty quickly grabbed the muffin off the ground and retreated back down the alley, toward her grandma's house: her heart racing and her pits sweating, releasing a strong and disgusting aroma.

CHAPTER FOUR

-

Misty was awoken early with a slam.

The movers had dropped the air mattress down on the front lawn, with Misty still sleeping on top of it. As she rubbed the sleep from her eyes, a moving van rolled off down the street.

Misty heard a high-pitched car horn. From the driveway, Grammy leaned out the window of the Mazda Miata.

"We're heading out, Misty, baby! Wish us luck on our drive! Come visit!"

Chip Jizzlin smiled behind the driver's seat. "Just make sure you knock before you come in!"

"Oh, Chip!" Grammy giggled.

"I can't visit while I'm on parole! I'm legally not allowed to leave the state! Jesus!" Misty pulled her blanket over her head.

"Well, be a good girl and come visit when parole's up. It looks like the weather's starting to get cold so we better get a move on down to the hot tub capital of the world! And you better start looking for a job, little lady--you have rent to pay!"

Misty flipped her grandma the bird as the Miata sped off down the street after the moving van.

"Well, shit." Misty thought. "'Start looking for a job.' Like it's that easy?"

It was early and Misty was cold and locked out of her old house. She contemplated spending the rest of the day at Walmart, when suddenly, a vision of the lifeless corpse lying cold in a dark alley flashed into Misty's head.

"Fuck! That really happened, didn't it?" Misty was filled with dread, panic and anxiety. Partially at the horror she'd witnessed and mostly at the fact that she had witnessed it. The last thing she needed was to be caught at the scene of a crime one day after being released on parole.

"No one saw me there, it's okay," Misty thought. "There was no one else in the coffee shop and there was no one in the alley. In fact, I could show up there today and no one would even be any the wiser. But I don't need coffee, I need a job."

The cafe was clearly abuzz as the bell on the front door jingled and Misty walked in. The morning customers didn't seem at all deterred by the presence of what appeared to be a police investigation going on around them. Misty approached the counter.

"Hello. Misty Cheevis, I have an interview here today."

The barista this morning had a much different demeanor than the deceased barista from the night before. Tall and lanky, the barista was wearing her apron over a polka-dotted blouse and a long green skirt. She maneuvered around the shop at a much quicker pace, bouncing around like a felt puppet on Sesame Street.

"Oh, my gosh. An interview? What? Oh, my. Okay... give me a couple minutes--okay, okay, okay, okay, okay... Quad Latte for here!" The barista shouted extremely loudly over the sound of steaming milk. "You want anything to drink!?" She screamed again, but caught herself after she realized Misty was right in front of her, no reason to scream. "Sorry," she continued at a normal volume, "can I get you anything while you wait?"

"Nah..."

"Good!" Relieved, the quirky barista winked at Misty, thinking she had said "no" because she was aware of how busy the barista was. In reality, Misty didn't like coffee and the hot chocolate from the night before was not worth the price.

Misty took a seat at an empty table with a slight view behind the counter, into the back room. There were a handful of police officers milling around, taking photos and evidence. Another, tall, round, bald-headed officer sat at the counter carefully peeling open a cupcake.

Misty felt a little bit nervous, with the cops milling about. But the fact that they hadn't bothered her, yet, made her feel like she was in good shape. And the important thing was that this coffee shop obviously needed an employee, and from the looks of it, they could use help quick.

The barista eventually was able to get all the drinks served. She glanced at the door and then took a deep breath and joined Misty at her table.

"Hi, my name is Summer Singh. I'm the assistant manager here... well, actually, I guess I'm the manager here, now."

Summer smiled awkwardly and scratched her straight black hair, cut into a bob. It complemented her angular features.

"Oops," she said, as she recognized she had just touched her hair. She took out a small bottle of sanitizer from her skirt pocket and squeezed it into her hands.

"Hi, I'm Misty."

"Now, you said you have an interview here?" Summer asked, applying a squeeze of gel to her hands, continuing to rub.

"Yep."

"Vanessa must have scheduled that before... before... Oh, never mind. Anyway, do you have coffee experience?"

Misty decided to just make some shit up. It's just coffee. How hard could it be?

"Yeah, I used to work at Coffee Star in Parma. It's a chain, though, so it might be different from how you do things, here."

Summer's eyes darted around the shop, quickly, assessing if anyone needed her help. Her fingers tapped on the table.

"Well, are you a fast learner?"

"Oh, yeah. I pick things up real quick. Learned how to change a flat when I was seven years old. Learned how to drive when I was six."

"Hah!" Summer appreciated what she perceived to be Misty's "sense of humor."

"Honestly," Summer said, "Between you and me, being a barista isn't really all that hard. Sure, we take it seriously here and we care about the product, but right now I'm just looking for someone who can make the drinks and keep on top of everything: dishes, brewing coffee, ring 'em out, you know. And hopefully have a good attitude while doing it."

Misty was a little scared about the attitude part. Attitude, she'd been told, was an area where she "needed work."

"Heh. Yeah, yeah. I can do all that." Misty tried to act as professional as possible, forcing out an awkward closed-mouth smile.

The bell on the door rang again as a group of four women walked into the shop. Summer rolled her eyes and looked back at Misty.

"Can you start now?"

Misty eyed the pastry case that she'd noticed when she came in. "Yeah, I kinda haven't had breakfast, yet, so...."

"Grab a muffin and I'll show you how to operate the register."

Misty joined Summer behind the counter for the next wave of customers. She helped restock supplies and poured milk for Summer to steam. Summer was much nicer than the barista from the night before. The one who had been murdered.

While they were busy working and buzzing around behind the counter getting drinks prepared, Summer informed Misty that they were actually kind of desperate for help.

"Vanessa, may she rest in peace--terrible thing that happened... and I'm not trashing her--I wouldn't trash a dead person--but I have to say she prematurely fired an employee last week and we've been strapped ever since. Working doubles, almost creeping into overtime, which is not allowed under any circumstances or upper management will get pissed. So, I'm actually complimenting Vanessa, it's great that she finally set up an interview. I just wish she'd have told me."

"Yeah, she said you guys needed someone quick. Luckily, I'm pretty open, don't have much else on my plate right now."

"So you can open tomorrow?" Summer asked, nervously.

The uniformed man at the counter picked the last few individual crumbs off of his plate before slowly standing up from the stool at the counter, letting out a big grunt. He ambled to the back room.

"It looks like we might need some more lids, Misty," Summer called out from the front of the shop.

"Lids. Yeah. I'll grab 'em." Misty snuck into the back room. The door to the alley was open a crack. She could see yellow tape blocking off the crime scene and she could hear one of the police officers addressing the bald man.

"Well, detective, we've collected all the evidence we could gather. Nothing conclusive. You already know about the boxcutter, but there were no fingerprints on it."

"We got what we could," the large detective responded. "Don't worry about it. No one slices someone's throat and gets away with it. We'll track 'em down. Hell, we'll track down everyone who was in the area last night and I promise you, someone will know something."

Misty's armpits got really hot and started to sweat.

"So, the garbage men discovered her on their route this morning, huh? That must've been shocking," said one of the police officers as he shook his head.

"I recognized her when I showed up," the detective responded. "I come in here every once in a while. I hit up all the shops. She wasn't the nicest barista. Never gave us free coffee, only half off. Could just smell the insubordination on her."

"Woah," Misty thought to herself. Sure the barista was kind of a bitch to Misty, too, but she wasn't investigating her murder. What a hater!

"So tell me what we know, officer." The detective lit a cigarette. Misty could smell the smoke as it wafted through the open door and into the back room, where she pretended to look for lids. The police officer took out his notebook and caught the detective up to speed.

"Like I said, there were no fingerprints on the boxcutter. The back door to the shop was left open all night, but there was no money taken from the safe. The cash was still in the register, which was locked when the employee arrived this morning, which she says is suspicious. Apparently the victim didn't socialize with her coworkers and didn't reveal much to them about her life. Her parents are separated. Dad's in Florida and the mom's in Indiana. She asked if we would cremate the body and send it to her."

"Hah. Yeah, right. She think we're Amazon or something?" the detective threw his cigarette on the ground and stomped it out. "See if anyone in the neighborhood noticed anything suspicious last night. Unfortunately there are no cameras around here. Most of these small businesses are too cheap to invest in security."

"Well, that's a relief. Hopefully they don't investigate too seriously," Misty thought.

"That cupcake made me hungry. Let's hit up Shelly's Diner and get out of here," concluded the detective.

Misty hustled out of the back room and returned to the counter, where she stacked lids on the table that held the cream and sugar and napkins and straws.

"Sorry that took so long," Misty apologized.

"Oh, it's okay," Summer responded. "Now that we don't have a box cutter it takes a little longer to open the boxes."

The detective made his way out of the back room.

"Who's this by the way?" he asked loudly.

"Oh, yes, this is actually our newest employee, Misty."

"Last name?" He looked directly at Misty. He was hairless—like a naked mole rat. His sandy skin was dry—like a naked mole rat's habitat.

"Cheevis."

"I have to get everyone's names. I don't know if you've been informed but a crime was committed here last night. A murder. We're doing everything we can to investigate and to make sure you're all safe here at the Coffee Bucket." He slammed his hand on the table a couple of times, in a "that's that," manner.

"Thanks, Detective Mills," Summer responded. "You want to take a coffee with you?"

"Sure, gimme three of 'em, will ya?"

The pace slowed down as morning turned into afternoon and as it did, Summer began to lighten up a little bit. She showed Misty how to start cleaning up the cafe, preparing it to be closed.

"I like to sing a clean-up song to make the work a little more fun," she said, after which she began to sing her own made-up song about cleaning.

"Spray a little, scrub a little, wipe a little, woo! Clean up, clean up, that is whatcha do! Sing it with me, Misty! Spray a little, scrub a little..."

She also told Misty that they'd fill out paperwork the next afternoon, to make the hiring official.

"Official." Misty liked the sound of that.

"Unfortunately, we're going to have to close early tonight. We don't have anyone to work until close, it's just you and me manning the ship now, matey. Ahoy! I'm the captain and I have a peg leg! Argh. Me peg leg clanking on the planks, driving me bonkers! Hah! I'll find someone else soon, I'm just glad Vanessa found you or else today would have been a real stinker. I think I'll let you go home and get some rest and I can finish up here. Will you be able to open the shop tomorrow?"

"Yeah, sure. Whatever."

"Perfect! I'm going to run to the back to count the drawer. If you need me I'll be in the office, knock before you enter okay! I'm kind of a nervous nelly!"

Summer went to the back room, leaving Misty alone in the cafe. It was getting dark and Misty felt a chill up her spine. The bell on the door rang and in walked a short person in a black hoodie and wide leg blue jeans with rips in them.

Summer had greeted most of the customers all day, so Misty's voice sounded awkward and robotic as she welcomed the person to the cafe.

"Hello. Hi, how are you, today—tonight. This evening."

"I'm... okay... is Vanessa working today?" The person's voice was quiet and raspy.

Misty's stomach twisted into a knot. She didn't know what to say.

"Um.. No. She's not working today. Were you friends with Vanessa?"

"What do you mean 'were you friends?'" The customer's head turned up, slightly. Dark brown eyes peered out from underneath. "I mean, yes. Yes, we are friends... at least, I guess you could say that."

"Oh. Okay." Misty just stood there. What should she do? Was it her job to tell everyone that Vanessa was dead? She wasn't a doctor!

"What's going on? Is everything okay? She didn't show up at D&D last night, either. I was worried!"

"D&D?" Misty asked.

"Dungeons and Dragons. A group of us play every Thursday night. Vanessa didn't show up last night and she didn't let any of us know why and she hasn't responded to any of our messages. Do you know what's going on?"

"She dead," Misty said, bluntly.

The person in the hood stood still and continued to stare at the ground. The room grew cold and silent. Suddenly the person in the black hoodie ran to the front door and shoved it open, the bell slamming against the glass. They rushed out into the darkness as the door came to a shut, with an ominous jingle.

CHAPTER FIVE

-

THAT EVENING MISTY DROVE AROUND a little bit looking for "For Rent" signs. All the large buildings that she contacted had long application processes that she was nervous to submit to. To Misty, it shouldn't be so hard.

"I give you money, you let me sleep there... am I missing something?"

She didn't want to submit an application. Maybe someone could get murdered and she could just take their apartment, she thought to herself, with only a little bit of shame.

Her old Corolla rattled past her grandma's old house. No one was even living there. It was empty. A sign in the front yard announced that it was owned by "Premier Property Development" and said "NO TRESPASSING."

Misty didn't want to trespass, but she did want to tear down the sign in the front yard. She grabbed a tricycle from the neighbor's driveway. From the legal positioning of the public sidewalk, she hurled the tricycle at the sign, smashing it into the ground.

She returned to a parking spot in front of the coffee shop and turned off the car, slowly drifting off into as deep a sleep as she could muster in the small four-door sedan.

Misty was awoken from her sleep by a knock on the driver's side window of her car.

"Hello? Hello? Hi!"

A woman stared calmly at Misty through the window, illuminated by a streetlight above.

"You gonna open the shop?"

"What?" Misty groggily wiped her eyes and yawned. She looked around and realized she was in front of the coffee shop. It was still dark out. "Shit. What time is it?"

"6:45." The shop was supposed to open at six.

"Fuck." Misty laid her head back on the headrest for just a moment before opening the door and stepping out of the car.

"I saw you working yesterday and figured you were here to open the shop but it looks like you dozed off, there."

The woman seemed friendly enough, seemed middle aged and was incredibly beautiful and made up. Lavender eyeshadow lightly dusted her warm copper skin and her lips were highlighted in a light pink. She had long, straight purple hair and wore a lacey yellow top that accentuated her curves and camouflage leggings that would conceal her lower half in the wild during hunting season. Misty liked what she saw.

"Yeah, yeah. I got here early and fell asleep."

The woman followed Misty to the front door of the coffee shop, a pleasant aroma wafting off her in the cool morning air.

"It's okay, I haven't seen any other customers come by yet, so you didn't lose any business. But our AA group always meets here on Friday mornings, so I figured you might need to get the coffee started and whatnot. Anyway, my name's Tramaine. What's your name?"

"Misty." She fumbled with the keys to the shop and eventually let herself in. Tramaine followed behind her.

"Oh, wow. Very cool name. Misty. Like the weather. Tramaine means 'big town made of stone.'"

"Okay," Misty replied. She looked around the shop. It was still dark. The lights switched on, startling Misty. She turned and noticed Tramaine standing by the lightswitch, wearing a slight grin.

Misty made her way behind the counter and looked around. Summer had shown her how to open the day before, but Misty was tired and also she didn't take notes or anything. Misty stood there with literally no idea of where to begin.

"I'd start by grinding the beans and brewing up a pot of coffee," Tramaine offered, sitting at the counter.

"Oh, right. I knew that," Misty responded, still standing there.

After a moment Tramaine pointed to the bag of beans beside the grinder, her manicured nails dazzling under the industrial lightbulb that hung from the ceiling. Misty opened the bag and measured out the coffee.

"There ya go, hun," Tramaine said cheerfully.

Together, Tramaine and Misty got the shop prepared for the AA group, which started to trickle in, leaving Misty to manage by herself. It wasn't easy and she definitely was screwing things up quite a bit. She was sweeping up two pounds of coffee beans that she spilled on the ground after she held an open bag upside down, when two men walked in the front door.

"Hello, there! Jerry Landollfi, of Simbiox Asset Management," the shorter man announced as they walked in, extending his hand to Misty. He was balding and had a pale, red face.

"This is my assistant, Jeff," he continued, nodding to the second, younger man, who was tall and large and looked like a Mormon college athlete.

Both men were dressed almost identically in khakis, a button down shirt and a fleece vest. Jerry sat in the last seat available at the counter and Jeff loomed behind him.

"We hear there's a new employee here!" Jerry said with a greater enthusiasm than Misty herself had ever possibly experienced.

"Really? Oh, yeah. That's me. Misty." Misty realized they must be here to get her signed up for her paperwork. Official.

"Wonderful," Jeff said, with a smile. He had a much calmer demeanor than his superior, Jerry. "You'll be happy to hear that your employer offers a retirement plan through Simbiox. It's a very generous plan and your employer will match up to five percent."

"Oh. That's cool," Misty said, having no idea what the man meant.

"Free money," Jerry added in a deep, reassuring voice.

Free money. Misty couldn't argue with that. And a retirement plan with "matching" did sound nice and official and grown up. Pizza Fever certainly didn't offer a retirement plan. All they offered was 20% off a large pizza on weekdays once a week. But Misty wasn't supposed to dwell on the past, it was time to think about her future.

She looked at the folder that Jerry held in his hands. Simbiox Asset Management. Misty was finally growing up and everyone else could suck it.

Jeff looked to his assistant, who had already pulled the paperwork from his briefcase. Misty turned to grab a pen from the jar by the cash register when she noticed Detective Mills walk in the front door.

"Welcome to Coffee Bucket. What can I get for you?" Misty asked.

"Yeah, just gimme a coffee," he said, continuing to stand there.

Misty didn't know if she should charge him. Based on what she'd overheard the day before, it seemed like the deceased barista charged them half price and some baristas didn't charge them at all. But Misty hadn't heard anything officially about the process and she didn't particularly like this man, so she poured him the coffee and typed the price into the register as she would any other customer.

"That'll be $2.50."

Detective Mills sighed and laboriously reached into his back pocket, struggling to wiggle his wallet out from the spot between his fat ass and his tight uniform. He gave her $3.

"Keep the change," he said. The counter was full, so he just squeezed in an open spot while other customers sipped their drinks and worked on their computers or read their newspapers.

"How is everything going around here? Any more trouble?" Detective Mills asked.

"I've just been here since this morning, I don't know. We closed early yesterday, anyway." Another customer had come in and Misty took their order and made their drink, giving a knowing shrug to Jerry and Jeff that she'd be over to sign the paperwork when she finished.

"Are you curious about the investigation?" the detective inquired as Misty measured out a chai latte.

Was Misty curious about the investigation? She certainly was! Her hope was that they found the murderer and she wouldn't have to panic about being in the wrong place at the wrong time. But she also wanted to play it cool, because she really had been in the wrong place at the wrong time.

"Oh yeah, the investigation. How is that going?"

"It's going well," He said loudly, so the entire cafe could hear. "The investigation into the murder is going well! You know it's important to get a fast start on a case like this. With every passing day, it gets harder to find the killer. So I ordered my men to canvass the neighborhood and speak with all the shop owners."

"Wow, it's a relief to hear you're on top of it, sir," said Jerry.

"Thank you, officer," Jeff agreed.

"It's my pleasure, good citizens. It's why I got into service in the first place. To bring justice to the community and that is what I will do with this case. Which is why I'm thrilled to inform you that several of the business owners we spoke to in the area claim to have encountered a strange person in their shop on the night of the murder."

Misty stopped wiping the wet mug she had just washed. Her heart sank and then began to pound. A strange woman in the area on the night of the murder? She had visited every shop on the street that night.

Detective Mills continued sharing his information. "A kind of deranged woman some of the shops say--"

"Deranged woman?" Misty said, shocked. She wasn't frightened; she was offended.

"Yes. Deranged man others say--"

Misty dropped the mug on the floor and it loudly bounced under the counter, but didn't break. Misty knelt down to pick it up, taking her time to hide and take a deep breath. It was her. She was the prime suspect.

"Apparently whoever it was, was asking weird questions about background checks, breaking merchandise and whatnot. Many of them felt disturbed and thought the person to be suspicious."

"I'll say," piped up a construction worker sitting at the counter finishing up his hot chocolate.

"Sounds like that's your guy," said a retired teacher, also at the counter.

"Someone in the area the night of the murder? Yep, they did it," agreed Jerry, who had been enthralled by the story.

Misty stood up from underneath the counter in time to see calm Jeff nodding in agreement.

"Case closed," agreed the dog-walker who had just walked in to hear the end of the conversation. "Got 'em!"

"Woof," barked the goldendoodle, in agreement.

Misty stood behind the counter, the towel squeaking as she continued to rub the dry mug with a little too much force.

"You know," the detective continued for all to hear, "let this be a lesson to you all. If these shopkeepers would have just done their due diligence and called the cops we probably wouldn't be tracking down a murderer right now, we'd just have someone in jail for trespassing."

"Tracking down?" Misty thought to herself. "They're looking for me."

"Welp, I've got a date with the Turlet," the detective slammed his empty cup on the counter and turned to the dog walker. "Best toilet in the neighborhood. I just feel so comfortable in there. Anyone wanna squeeze in before me? You're not gonna want to go after--HA! I can promise you that!"

Misty felt sick. Partly because she was imagining the damage the detective was gonna do to the bathroom, which she was responsible for cleaning at the shift change. But foremost, she was concerned about her own well-being. If she got involved in this crime it could put her whole situation in jeopardy. Sure, she didn't have all that much to lose, but what she had, she wanted to hold on to: her freedom.

From the sounds of it, she was the prime suspect, and she didn't have an alibi. Also, from what she's heard come out of this detective's mouth, she wasn't confident in his ability to correctly solve the case. In fact, with all the evidence that pointed to Misty, it was hard to believe that he wouldn't just up and stop the investigation after arresting her as a suspect. He may not have had a strong case for her guilt, but she couldn't say she had a strong case for her innocence.

Misty couldn't concentrate as Jerry explained the retirement plan to her and she hadn't gotten a great night's sleep the night before. So she had a weird mixture of swinging in between falling asleep and raging at the injustice of the situation, compounded by the aggravation at having no idea what the retirement guys were talking about magnified by the frustration of getting interrupted by customers every few minutes. Misty really wanted to get signed up and become "official," but physically and mentally it was beyond her capabilities.

She was teetering in between drifting off and screaming at Jerry in frustration when the door once again opened and Summer walked in to replace her for the closing shift.

"Thanks so much for opening this morning, Misty. Did everything go alright?" Summer unlocked the back office and went in, hanging up her coat. She was wearing overalls, a cat sweatshirt and combat boots.

"Yeah, it was awesome!" Misty decided not to reveal that she opened an hour late or to pass along the information she'd learned from the detective. "Um, actually, I'm supposed to sign up for retirement with Jerry and Jeff and stuff?"

"Oh, my gosh! I totally forgot to get your paperwork from the main office this morning! You're not even on payroll, yet--you can't sign up for the retirement plan. I'm so sorry, guys."

Summer shrugged and looked toward Jerry and Jeff. "Can you guys come back another day? I'm so sorry."

Jerry and Jeff agreed, begrudgingly. They were very excited about this opportunity for Misty. And Misty was, too. But in a way, Misty was relieved. She hated paperwork: it reminded her of all the legal documents she had to sign before going to jail.

"Jail," Misty thought. Two days out and she was the prime suspect in a murder. It was hard for her not to become dejected and cynical. "What's the point of signing these papers? What's the point of growing up? I'm just going to be wrongfully accused of a crime, again."

Summer woke Misty up from her hazed out daze.

"Misty! I'm so sorry, I totally forgot to get the paperwork! I'm just really spazzed out lately with all that's going on. Hey, but the good news is that since you're not on payroll..." Summer grabbed Misty's hand and walked her to the back room and through a door to the manager's office. "...You get paid in cash today!"

Summer cautiously opened a cabinet door, just slightly. In her hand was a bundle of keys and about seven different keychains. Little animals, purses, a hand sanitizer keychain and more dangled from the keys.

"So they're harder to lose," Summer explained.

She knelt down and dialed the combination on the small safe that

Misty could see through the crack in the door. Summer made robot noises as she entered the combination: beep, boop, merrrrrrp, tssssss.

"Access granted," she stated in a robotic voice.

The dollar bills shimmered like pure solid gold in Misty's eyes and Summer pulled them from the money box inside the safe.

"Thanks for opening on such short notice, by the way," Summer said as she counted out the payment. "I really appreciate you being so quick to help out. I know you had to be up early, so you can leave now, if you want. Unless you have any questions for me first."

Misty was grateful that she could leave. She went to the back room to grab her coat. Misty didn't have any questions for Summer. She had questions, sure. How am I going to get off the hook for this murder? Should I have even taken this job? Where am I going to live? If they're looking for me, they're not looking for the actual murderer.

Misty had a headache. She was sweating from the stress as she walked out of the back room with her coat dragging on the floor behind her. The pathetic sight made Summer feel guilty at having Misty open on such short notice.

"Misty," she said. "Thanks, again, for your help. You know, we would normally have two other employees here to help out, but Vanessa is, well, you know... gone and unfortunately, she fired Bart abruptly last week."

Misty's ears perked up. "Vanessa fired someone? Who's Bart Abruptly?"

"It means she just fired him without warning any of us. It was weird. We were all pretty annoyed by it, because she just up and fired him without hiring anyone first, but... whatever. It's hard to be mad at her, now, I guess. I'm sorry we're short staffed, but the good news is I'm interviewing someone this afternoon, so fingers crossed we'll be back to fully staffed tomorrow."

Misty didn't really care about being fully staffed, but the news that Vanessa had suddenly fired someone piqued Misty's interest. She had to find out more about who this person was and why Vanessa had to get rid of them. Misty may have been the detective's primary suspect, but now Misty had a suspect of her own.

CHAPTER SIX

-

THE NAME OF THE EMPLOYEE was Bartholemew Reyes. Also known as Bart.

Misty didn't want to seem too suspicious, so she didn't ask Summer for his phone number or anything. She did inquire as to whether or not Summer knew where Bart went to work.

"I don't know," Summer said, while stocking the fridge with fresh boxes of almond milk. "Some kind of office job. Action Systems? Data Illusions? CorpCorp Limited? The name was very much not memorable."

"Do you know what the job was?" Misty asked.

"I don't even think Bart knew what the job was. I asked if he could describe it and he just said a bunch of buzz words like 'accounts' and 'access' and 'immersion' and 'such as.'" Summer looked up from her work. "He kept saying, 'such as.' And then I found myself saying 'such as' a lot, as well, such as."

Misty wanted to track this guy down. If he revenge murdered Vanessa or killed her for some personal beef, then he was going to have to take the blame. Not Misty!

"Action Systems?"

Misty approached the cash register, which was operated by an iPad. When Summer excused herself to the office to set up the cash drawer for the next day, Misty opened the web browser and did a search.

She typed in "Action Systems," but couldn't find any businesses with that name. She tried "Data Illusions" and "CorpCorp Limited," but they also returned zero results, though the search engine did recommend a photography studio that did custom glamor shots called "Illusions Unlimited."

The door chimed. A woman with large breasts came in and ordered a breve half-caf latte. Misty was angry that the woman had interrupted her search.

"Stupid lady with her huge tits. Stupid ass," she thought to herself.

Misty couldn't stop peering at the woman's breasts.

"Jugs. That's what those are. Jugs... "

Misty drifted off, recalling the time she checked Dustin's browser history on his computer and found over 1,000 hits for "Huge Jugs" porn videos.

Misty stopped steaming the milk and slammed down the milk pitcher: "That's it!"

Misty quickly poured the woman her drink and passed it off. "Thank you, miss. You're looking good."

"Thanks, babe," the lady said as she turned and left the shop.

Misty returned to the iPad. There had to be a chance that Bart had used the work computer to either look for jobs or research companies with openings. She scrolled through the browser history: possum memes... gun show... sentient robots...huge jugs... (to brew iced tea in)...

Eventually she came across it: "Account Manager -- Job Opening."

She contacted the number on the site and they mentioned that the position had already been filled.

"Gotcha," Misty said.

NubCorp Accesslink SysTech Limited was located in a corporate park in Independence, Ohio, a suburb along the Cuyahoga River, just outside Cleveland's borders. The city offered businesses strong incentives to operate in its municipality, resulting in it being populated less with homes and neighborhoods, and more with office buildings, parking lots and food chains with lunch specials.

The office park that NubCorp was located in consisted of three identical glass buildings, each four stories high. Misty searched for building #3 and took the elevator to the second floor.

Inside it was quiet, the only sound the droning of the fluorescent lights. Misty hated it. It reminded her of jail. Sure, jail didn't have large windows to the outside, but the air was just stale.

She found the door to NubCorp and knocked. There was no answer, so Misty peered through the glass panel to the right of the door. Through the blinds she could see people sitting at desks, all with their headphones on.

Misty let herself in and approached the nearest cubicle.

"Hey," she said. "Hello?"

The woman at the computer was intensely reading "Star Panties," a gossip website.

"Yo!" Misty waved her hand in the woman's peripheral vision.

"AH!" The woman let out a scream. "Oh, God. Sorry. You scared me."

The employee took a moment to collect herself. She held her hand on her chest and took deep breaths. She was wearing an olive-colored cardigan and a necklace with a cross on it.

"Geez, I'm not a ghost, lady," Misty said.

"I'm sorry. You just really snuck up on me there. We don't get a lot of visitors up here. We don't even have a receptionist actually. My desk just happens to be closest to the door. But this isn't one of my responsibilities, in fact."

Misty wasn't concerned with the floor plan of the office and individual job descriptions. She was here on business.

"I'm here to see Bart Reyes."

"Who?"

"Bart Reyes."

"Bart?" The woman chuckled. "Who's Bart?"

She leaned her head outside her cube. "Helen! Who's Bart?"

A woman leaned her head out of a nearby cube. "Bart? Girl, I don't know. I'm not the receptionist!"

"Neither am I!" the woman responded aggressively.

"Bart? Is that the new guy?" An older man's voice lifted out of a cubicle down the row.

"No, the new guy is 'BJ,'" responded yet another person, who's bespectacled eyes could be seen peering over the top of a room divider.

"Do you mean BJ?" the woman who was not the receptionist asked.

"I mean Bart!" Misty was officially annoyed. What was going on around here?

The woman shrugged, popped a piece of Trident in her mouth, put her headphones back on and returned to reading about the latest celebrity syphilis scare. Misty was fuming. What a waste.

The pair of glasses peered over the divider once more. "Does Bart ever go by BJ?"

Misty was just about to curse this person out, but she stopped and considered it. "BJ?" It was worth a try. A hand with fingerless gloves lifted itself out of the cube and pointed Misty toward another room off to the back and side of this first space.

The room was large and not particularly full. But there were enough people and specifically enough young men in business casual, that it was impossible for Misty to guess which one was Bart. She didn't want to waste any more time, so she just decided to shout.

"Bart!" She yelled at a loud enough volume to be heard through noise cancelling headphones.

A few hands pointed to a cubicle toward the back of the office where a short young man was slouching at his desk, giggling while staring at his phone.

"What's so funny, murderer?" Misty thought to herself. She was sure to make a lot of movement as she approached his desk, so as to not alarm him like she did the jittery lady in the other room.

"Hi. You Bart? Can we talk?"

Bart led Misty to a small meeting room with a round table and glaring lights overhead. The room had a glass wall exposing it to the rest of the office.

"I don't have a lot of meetings. This is exciting. We get free water for meetings. You one of my clients? I've never met a client before."

Bart grabbed two miniature bottles of Ice Mountain out of a miniature fridge that sat on a counter along the back wall. He was short and had an impressively sharp haircut, perfectly manicured. He looked good, even in business casual and Misty could notice the curves of his biceps underneath his tight oxford.

"No, I'm not a client."

"Oh," Bart looked out into the office. "Well, here, let's have the water anyway. Sit down. Let's look professional. What are you here about, then?"

"I'm here to talk about Coffee Bucket? You used to work there, right?"

Bart let out an audible groan.

"Ugh. The Bucket. Yeesh. Yeah I worked there."

"Before Vanessa fired you."

"Whoa, whoa, whoa. Who are you? Are you from corporate? Did you call Vanessa as a reference? I didn't list her as a reference. She said she fired me? Well, that is not the case. I quit Coffee Bucket. I was not fired."

"That's not what I heard?"

"What? What did you hear?" Bart was clearly uneasy. He kept taking sips of her water. Misty got excited, figuring she had him cornered. "This is so unfair." He took another sip of water.

"You got fired and then you were so mad that you murdered Vanessa."

Bart sprayed water all over Misty.

"Hey! What the hell, man?" Misty jumped up from her chair.

"Murdered!" Bart looked confused and almost amused. "Whoa, whoa, whoa. Who the hell are you?"

"I'm a friend of Vanessa's."

"And she was murdered?"

Bart grabbed some paper towels and wiped up the water off the table. Misty grabbed the towels out of his hand so she could wipe herself off.

"You bet she was murdered. Like you didn't know. Throat slit ear to ear. Sound familiar?"

"And you seriously believe I did it? Why would I murder Vanessa from Coffee Bucket?"

"Because she fired you! And you freaked out!"

"Oh, my God. You can't be serious, lady. I didn't care that I got fired. I already found a job anyway. I was just about to quit. She fired me because she learned I was about to quit and she was petty like that. And I'm pretty sure she wanted to sleep with me."

"Hah! I'm sure," Misty laughed. She hated guys like this. She'd slept with them before and it was always terrible.

"Look, I was happy to leave Coffee Fuck-It. I only wanted it to be a temporary job in the first place. I'm not cut out for service. I have a college degree. It just took me a while to find a real job—like an adult job. Why would I murder someone for firing me when I already had a better job lined up?"

College Degree. Real job. The words were hitting Misty hard. She was happy to be working at Coffee Bucket and for her that was a real job.

"In fact, I love it here. I don't have to suffer the humiliation of telling people I work at a coffee shop, now. I can tell them I'm an account manager at NubCorp AccessLink SysTech and they leave me alone. I have an adult job, just like everyone else. I have healthcare and PTO. And there's a Wii in the meeting room next to this one. And a ping-pong table in the break room. So it's actually pretty cool. They said they'd get me a standing desk if I want one, but I just bought a gaming chair, so I don't mind sitting."

Misty couldn't think of a response. He made a good point. Why would he be mad to stop working at a coffee shop? Especially if he had an adult job lined up. Misty wondered if she should start looking for an adult job.

"Actually," Bart seemed to be reminded of something. "When did you say she was murdered? Was it at night?"

"Thursday. Around the time Coffee Bucket closes."

"Hah! There we go. Come with me."

Misty and Bart took a trip back to his desk where he pulled up a video on the video game streaming website Twitch.

"See? That's me. BigDong92. This is a video replay of me playing Call of Duty on Thursday night."

The screen showed a screen from the popular video game. In the lower right hand corner was Bart's face with headphones on. He was screaming obscenities at the screen as he hunted down opponents in the game.

"I'm pretty good, huh? Headshot! Poggers!"

Misty continued to watch the video: Bart's character gets shot in the game and Bart rages out, throwing a temper tantrum and a can of

Monster Energy Drink at the wall behind him.

"Hah. Yeah, I'm kind of competitive," Bart admitted over the sound of various obscenities being screamed through the computer's speakers. "See, there's the timestamp. I streamed Thursday from 6pm to 11:30pm. 7,000 people can confirm."

Misty was a little disturbed and a lot defeated. It was a dead end. First of all, Misty didn't believe this little dweeb would have the balls to murder anyone in real life. He was busy playing games at night and fiddling around at work all day. Didn't seem to have the capacity or stakes in his life to really risk it all. He was lame. And more importantly, he had a solid alibi.

Bart sat back in his chair, chuckling as he finished admiring the clip of himself flipping out.

"Yeah, I have a lot of viewers. Thinking about going full time. I'd miss the benefits and the W-2 this job provides me, but streaming has its own rewards. People like watching me freak out. I think it makes me relatable: good looking guy, freaking out. A lot of people have rage issues, actually. You never know when someone might SNAP!"

He lunged at Misty playfully, startling her.

"Hah!"

"People like watching him rage out?" Misty thought to herself. She wondered why she never got that reaction when she raged out.

A middle-aged woman with a bob haircut approached Bart's desk.

"Oh, shit!" Bart closed the browser and pulled up an Excel spreadsheet. "My supervisor," he whispered to Misty.

"Bart."

"Hi, Trish. I was just showing one of my clients here some of the data protocol submission packages before EOD."

"Yeah, whatever. Listen, I just got word that we need to collate the ten-forty files for management resources and it needs to be done by EOD."

"Ugh!" Bart let out another groan. "I'm kind of busy here. Is there anyone else that can do it?"

"Bart, I'm busy, too. The Bazelbalm account just dumped a whole load of PTP's on my desk. I cannot do it."

"Well, I can't do it either! I'm swamped, Trish."

"Bart! Come on. I need you to do this."

"It's not fair. You always make me do it!"

Misty decided it was a good time to leave. With the sounds of the Trish and Bart bickering in the background, Misty decided maybe getting an "adult job" could wait. As a matter of fact, Misty had a real job. A full time job. Tracking down Vanessa's killer. And the only benefit that came with this job was the benefit of staying out of jail.

"...by EOD, Bart! I mean it!"

Misty heard Trish storm off as she made her way past the room with Wii and the ping-pong table, back to the room where the "non-receptionist" was located.

As she was leaving, Bart called out from behind her.

"Hey! So who's managing the coffee shop now, anyway? Is it Summer?"

"Yep."

"Hah. Maybe talk to her. She's a real weirdo, if you ask me. Everyone thought so. Just something off about her. And she was pretty critical of Vanessa. She was never satisfied with how Vanessa was running the company and always finding ways to bring it up to me, expecting me to agree with her. And from the looks of it, she had something to gain from having Vanessa out of the picture."

"The manager position."

"Yep. And another $2.50 an hour."

CHAPTER SEVEN

-

MISTY AWOKE TO THE TAPPING OF ACRYLIC NAILS on the driver's side window of her car.

"Shit. Hi, Tramaine." Misty waved and opened the door of the car out into the blustery fall morning air.

Tramaine accompanied Misty into the shop and sat at the counter as she got the place set up. After Misty filled the cash register and brewed the first pot of coffee, Misty stole a scone out of the pastry case and leaned on the counter in front of Tramaine.

"Girl, you need a place to stay?" Tramaine had caught on to Misty's situation.

"Why? Do I look bad?"

Tramaine, who looked like she belonged on the cover of Black & Sickening magazine just stared at her. Misty looked fucked up. Her hair was greasy and she smelled like old coffee and body odor and she was wearing the same clothes she'd been wearing for three days.

"What time you get off work?"

Misty agreed to go with Tramaine after work to look for apartments. It was time for her to get a place to stay. Misty didn't have time to spend all the cash she'd been getting at the end of her shifts, so she figured she should soon have enough money for the first month's rent.

Finding a place to stay might actually be pretty nice, Misty thought. And certainly grown up. But Misty had some other business to take care of first. Her and Summer's shift overlapped by half an hour, and Misty was planning on finding out some more information. Was it possible that Summer wanted the management job so bad that she would kill Vanessa? Summer was critical of how Vanessa was running the shop--did Summer just snap one day?

Misty needed to crack down on whoever did this and she was confident she could figure out who it was. If she crossed paths with the killer, Misty knew she'd be able to sniff the truth out of them--which was why she was desperate to give Summer the heat.

The morning was busy again and the coffee shop was full of customers. It was almost as if news of murder had increased people's interest in the coffee shop. Most of the customers inquired about the progress on the case, and many hoped to be in the cafe when the detective came around.

Misty was still new to the job and she was also easily frustrated. Plus, Jerry and Jeff, the retirement guys, had shown up again to go over the retirement plan with Misty. It was hard for her to manage all the tasks at once.

She accidentally gave whole milk to an almond milk customer, made an americano for someone who wanted a cappuccino and gave someone a mocha without any espresso in it. She forgot some orders entirely, all because she was busy running fantasy interrogations in her mind with her coworker killer.

By the time Summer came in for the shift change, Misty was dripping with sweat and shaking. Summer had barely set down her stuff when Misty pulled up close, heat and moisture radiating off her musty body.

"Howdy pardner," Summer said as she set her stuff down on the counter. She was wearing cowboy boots, a cowboy hat and a red, white and blue jacket with gold fringe on it. "Busy morning?"

"Why? Are you unsatisfied with my work like you were Vanessa's?"

Summer, who was shuffling through her purse, stood upright and looked at Misty.

"Now what would make you think that? Orbitz?" She handed Misty a piece of gum. "It just looks like you've been working hard in here, that's all. And I appreciate it! I know how busy mornings can get. Howdy, fellas. Hope y'all aren't drinking too much in my here saloon, ya' hear?"

Jerry and Jeff were seated at the counter.

"Hi, Summer. Have you gotten Misty on payroll, yet? We were just explaining the program again to her today and we'd love to get her signed up."

"I brought her paperwork to fill out today when we have a second. And guess who's coming in later? Our newest employee! I hired someone last night. It's going to make our lives a lot easier, Misty. But, I do want to get this place tidied up a bit before we dive into any paperwork. It looks like it was a busy morning."

"Why do you keep saying that? Critical of my work? Reminding you of Vanessa's or something?"

Summer began wiping down the counters and putting away miscellaneous dishes. "I am just mentioning that it looks like it was busy. It's busy a lot! You keep bringing up Vanessa. What's going on?"

"I talked to Bart. He said you and Vanessa didn't get along."

Summer paused her task for a moment, gathering her thoughts. Misty wasn't sure if she was going to answer and she knew she was maybe pushing a little too far, but eventually Summer let a little out.

"I'll be honest. Only because I'd like to share with you what I expect from a manager, so you know what you can expect from me."

"Whatever, just spill the beans, lady," Misty thought.

"This job isn't hard. Sometimes the job is so easy that there's a temptation to get distracted by nonsense that either isn't important or doesn't involve you."

Summer paused, expecting Misty to figure out this last statement was in reference to her gossiping about the drama between Summer and Vanessa. It wasn't clear Misty was going to figure that out, so Summer continued.

"Vanessa was distracted. She was discontent. And her mind was elsewhere. It felt to me like she had already moved on from this job--like how Bart acted once he started looking for jobs. I guess some people can't do this work for a long time and I get it. But the manager should be fine doing the work. She should be on top of things. Again, it isn't a difficult job. But Vanessa neglected her responsibilities and, yes, that got on my nerves! I didn't decide to work at a coffee shop because I was looking for a challenge! I'm here to enjoy myself! It should be easy!"

"Do you know if she had another job or was looking for one?"

"I don't know what her career plans were. But she always seemed stressed out--literally always. Which I can also understand. Everyone has a personal life and I know she had broken up with her boyfriend recently. And he's a prick, like we all knew that."

"Vanessa had an ex-boyfriend?" Misty's ears perked up. "I have an ex-boyfriend and I want to kill him. Maybe Vanessa's ex wanted to kill her!"

"You know, maybe Vanessa had a personal health issue that distracted her," Summer pondered. "We don't get paid a lot and we don't have healthcare. Luckily the company is setting up a retirement plan, but for the most part it isn't the easiest job to live off of."

"But as manager, you got a raise, right? That would help make living off this job a little easier."

"It's true. I did get a raise. But the manager does more work." Summer grabbed an empty carafe and started a new batch of coffee. "But it's also not a demanding job, which is what I value about it. The days aren't stressful--well they shouldn't be. But working with Vanessa was stressful. Mostly because she didn't keep on top of things. And then she'd get mad when something went wrong! It was extremely frustrating."

Misty could tell Summer had strong feelings about this. She was pretty strict and straightforward regarding her values. Could it be that her work ethic was so strong that she decided to take things into her own hands and eliminate one of the problems? Everyone knew Summer was a strange bird. And she admitted that the barista wage isn't always the easiest to live off of. Misty wasn't writing off Summer as a suspect just yet.

Suddenly, the bell on the door rang and Misty and Summer both raised their heads to see who had entered.

Detective Mills strolled in lifting his pants up.

"Well, well, well..."

He made eye contact with Misty and she froze.

"If it isn't exactly the person I was looking for."

He strolled up to the counter and patted his hands on the surface. Misty pretended to be busy.

"Mrs. Cheevis. How are we this fine day?"

Misty looked up at the police officer, reluctantly. "I'm fine."

The detective patted his hands a few more times loudly on the counter.

"Got any plans for after work, Cheevis? Grocery shopping perhaps?"

"Uh... no." Misty was annoyed. Why was this guy acting so annoying?

"Where do you do your grocery shopping these days? You ever try... Aldi?"

"Yeah, I been to Aldi," Misty responded. "Why--"

Misty was wondering why he was curious about her shopping routine.

"I love Aldi," Jerry piped in.

"Me, too," added Jeff. "I have an Aldi keychain that lets you keep a quarter in it! Very efficient." He pulled out his keys and showed off his keychain.

The detective stared down Misty, grinning like a psychopath.

"Are you a believer in coincidences, Summer?" He asked, still staring at Misty.

"I believe in astrology, psychics and Reiki massage. Nothing is a coincidence," Summer responded.

"Oh, really. You hear that Cheevis? So then, Summer, what would you think if I told you that an individual close to the crime that occurred right here last week, had been released from jail less than 48 hours prior to the crime being committed. Coincidence?"

Summer squinted her eyes and took a minute to translate the confusing language that the detective was trying to use.

"Well, I guess I'd be curious what they were in jail for in the first place and if that was related to the second crime that was committed."

"Assault," the detective said loudly. He then looked at Misty again, adding, "And stalking."

Misty's heart skipped another beat. "Damn it," she thought. "He looked my dumb ass up."

"Ahh...assault and stalking." Summer took in the new information. "That is suspect. I guess, before I decided if it was more than a coincidence, I'd wonder if this person had a prior relationship with the victim?"

"We're looking into that." The detective was quick to respond.

"I guess I'm also wondering how many people are released from jail in a day or in a week, because certainly other criminals would have been released prior to the crime being committed who should also be looked into if that's the criteria we're going on..."

"I don't have that information," Summer was proving to be a little too analytical for the detective's tastes. "I just think it's interesting that an individual who was just released from jail would find themselves in close proximity to another crime not shortly after they were released."

"Well, if they already had experience being in proximity to a crime wouldn't their chances of being in proximity to another crime actually be greater than your average person?"

"You know what, forget I asked!" The detective threw up his hands dismissively.

"I don't believe in coincidences but I don't really jump to conclusions either," Summer explained to Jerry and Jeff. "I'm just weird like that. I'm a Pisces."

"I, on the other hand," continued the detective, "am a detective. And I have a strong intuition that I'm onto something. I can feel it in my heartburn. When it flares up like this, I know I'm onto something." He winced and swallowed the acid reflux that had made its way up his esophagus.

"Good for you. I'm glad you're making progress on the case. I'm sure Vanessa's family is grateful as well," Summer said, genuinely.

"Thank you, Summer. You know her family didn't seem all that responsive, to be honest. Her dad's in Florida and her Mom's in Indiana. Didn't seem all that distraught about their kid's death. Terrible how the family structure has broken down these days. Anyway, Summer, if you ever feel unsafe here..." He looked at Misty, again. "If you're ever at all concerned for your safety, please don't hesitate to give us a call up at the station."

The detective reached behind him and pulled a rolled up manila envelope out of his pants and dropped it on the counter.

"Welp, duty calls!" he exclaimed, before scuttling to the bathroom.

Misty and Summer looked at the envelope.

"I don't want to touch that," Summer said with a look of concern. "He pulled it out of his pants."

"It looks moist," Misty agreed.

Nevertheless, the curiosity was more than Misty could handle. She opened the envelope. Inside was her police record and information about her arrest and criminal charges. She slid the papers over to Summer. Summer looked it over.

"This looks official. I can't read it. It makes no sense to me. But I can see it has your name on it. What is it?"

"It's my criminal record."

Misty shared her story with Summer. Every time she got loud or heated, Summer managed to quiet her down, so customers wouldn't overhear.

"Do you have to fire me?" Misty asked, recalling all the rejections she'd already received based on her record.

Summer took a deep breath.

"Are you still journaling?"

"Yes," Misty lied.

Just then the bathroom door opened and Detective Mills strolled out, drying his hands with a huge wad of paper towels. Misty started to collect her personal items in preparation to leave.

"Cheevis. I see you're still here. Summer, mind if I have a word with you?"

He leaned over the counter near Summer and spoke loud enough for everyone, including Misty, to hear.

"You know, given who is here on the premises, you may want to ensure your safety. For example, keep sharp and heavy blunt objects secured. Keep tabs on the boiling water. For your own safety. You know, even those sanitizer tablets you got by the dishwashing sink, I took a bottle to the bathroom with me for reading material. It says those things are strong enough to kill HIV. There's a lot of dangerous stuff around here. Be safe."

"Okay...," Summer muttered.

"Did you have time to look over those papers?"

"I did," She replied.

"Well, I hope you can find someone to fill Misty's spot promptly. It's a shame she withheld the truth from you, but what can you expect."

"I'm not firing Misty, thank you," Summer replied.

"Oh, really?"

"As long as she shows up on time, does her work and doesn't assault anyone, then I don't care about her past. She did her time."

Misty was relieved. The only reason she showed up on time was because she didn't have a bed to sleep in and the coffee shop had scones she could steal. But whatever.

"And you can't fire her if she hasn't been hired, yet," Jerry piped in, with a grin. He waved a manila folder of paperwork in his hand.

Misty felt a little better. It seemed like people here might be on her side. It wasn't something she was totally used to, but if it was true, she could learn to like it.

"If you say so," the detective looked pissed. "Whatever floats your boat. Call me if this one starts to exhibit any violent tendencies."

Misty was contemplating exhibiting some violent tendencies, but managed to hold them in until the detective left. She was seething, but Summer assured her that she was fine to work at the shop as long as she did her job and didn't cause any trouble.

Misty couldn't make any promises, but she agreed to the terms.

As Misty was preparing to leave for the day, Summer called her over to introduce her to the new employee.

"Misty, meet Mr. Larry!"

Mr. Larry was an elderly man who looked like he weighed about 90 pounds. He had thin, platinum white hair and huge glasses that magnified his eyes. He wore an oversized suit and a goofy grin.

"Nice to meet you, doll!"

Misty was shocked by the hire. It had been a long time since she'd even seen someone that old. But Summer made the decisions and she could tell Summer was proud of her hire as she noticed her beaming at the cute old man as she helped him put on his apron.

Misty excused herself outside, where Tramaine was waiting for her.

"You okay, sweetie? You look a little rough."

Misty didn't feel like explaining to Tramaine that she was the primary suspect in a murder case.

"Forget it. Where's this house you want to show me?"

"It's not far from here. Wanna grab some clean clothes and stuff? You can shower there if you want."

"Shower there?"

"Yeah. A place just opened up where I'm staying. It's called Harmonious Shores. It's a sober house for women."

"Sober house?" Misty groaned. "Fuck."

CHAPTER EIGHT

-

Misty didn't have a substance abuse problem. Which was great, considering the amount of trouble she got herself into all while completely sober. Specifically, Misty wasn't under the influence when she assaulted her former manager at the Aldi. Therefore, being sober was not a requirement for her parole. So, the idea of voluntarily living in a sober community was not appealing to Misty.

"Hell, no," she said as she stood in front of a depressed looking building on a side street within walking distance of Coffee Bucket.

The house had a patchy, brown front lawn and the Ford Thunderbird in the driveway wasn't the only thing propped up on cinder blocks. The unfinished front porch was also precariously reinforced, framing a front door that was partially boarded up with a piece of particle board.

"Oh, this isn't the sober house. Our house is in the back. This is where the caretakers lives," Tramaine said enthusiastically.

"Is he taking care of our house? Because he sure isn't taking care of this one. Shit!" Misty kicked an empty can of Monster energy drink down the driveway.

Tramaine guided Misty to a small, split-level cottage in the back. Some late fall flowers were still in bloom in a little garden in front of the house, scattered with dry fallen leaves. Wind chimes decorated the front stoop and the door was painted a cheery bright yellow. It was charming, warm and inviting.

Tramaine smiled. "What do you think?"

"Looks gay," Misty said. She wasn't really into the decorative arts.

Tramaine invited Misty inside. It was cozy. A woven throw adorned a plump couch. Doilies sat on the coffee table and paintings of Jesus were on the walls. Misty was reminded of her grandma's house. That elderly ho.

"So, Martha relapsed and drank a box of White Claws last week. She had to move out. That means a spot opened in the upstairs room, with me."

"With you?"

"Yeah, Martha was my bunkmate. Honestly a sweet girl. I feel bad for her, but she broke the rules."

Misty was feeling dejected. Was this the best she could do? When she left her grandma's house it wasn't so she could move into another grandma's house. And they seemed pretty strict about rules—something Misty was pretty much programmed to ignore. Tramaine led Misty into the kitchen.

"Hi, Joan!"

Joan was an elderly woman with huge breasts. She was peeling potatoes, wearing a tanktop and an apron over tanned, freckeld, buttery skin. She had short grey hair and glasses that magnified her eyes.

"Stuffed cabbage is in the oven. Who's that?" Her voice was loud and her tone abrasive.

"This is Misty. I'm thinking maybe she can take Martha's spot."

"Can you pick up after yourself?" Joan asked. Then she screamed loudly, "Because CHELSEA is having some trouble and can't stop leaving her shit all over the place!"

From a room down the hall came a raspy smoker's voice. "Choke on a corn cob, you old fart! I'll do it later!"

Tramaine took Misty down the hall to the downstairs bedroom, where Joan stayed with Chelsea. There was a line of masking tape dividing the room in two. One side was extremely tidy and the other side was messy. Chelsea lay on her bed looking at her phone which was blasting Metallica. She was rail thin, with frizzy, brown hair and an complexion like the inside of a lemon.

"Oh, hey," she said when she noticed Tramaine and Misty.

"Chelsea is a waitress at the Bob's Falafel on 65th."

"Damn right," Chelsea responded. "Don't ask for no discounts because I don't do that shit and it's cheap enough there as is."

Upstairs was Tramaine's bedroom. There was a bed on each side of the room. Tramaine's side was tidy and there was a desk with a little curtain around it and lots of pillows on her bed. The other side was empty, with nothing but a bed, a small desk and a dresser.

"It's not much, but the rent is cheap and we have a good time here. We're putting together a 1,000 piece puzzle of the Last Supper tonight if you want to join us."

Misty wasn't sure about all of this. Sure, she needed a place to stay and she needed it now. But she was supposed to be growing up, being on her own, not living at her grandma's house again. And the thought of doing Jesus puzzles for a good time wasn't really the lifestyle she was trying to live.

"I'll think about it."

"You can stay here tonight, if you want. I just don't want you sleeping in your car around here. Especially with a murderer in the neighborhood."

"Thanks," Misty said. Tramaine had a point. Misty's back was sore from trying to sleep in her car. "I don't get it, though. Aren't there regulations and stuff for this? I'm not an alcoholic or drug addict. Shouldn't a drug addict be staying here?"

Tramaine bit her lip and played with the buttons on her frilly blouse.

"Yes," Tramaine said, "There are rules. And you do need to be in recovery to stay here. But you need a place to stay and I need a roommate."

Tramaine had gone through three roommates in the last six months. Martha succumbed to a case of White Claws. Yolanda tried to steal Tramaine's cell phone and Bluetooth speakers. And Penelope wouldn't stop trying to recruit the rest of the house to become Jehovah's Witnesses.

Tramaine was desperate for a roommate that wouldn't compromise the living situation that she, Joan and Chelsea were trying to facilitate--a situation that worked for the three of them. She looked at the floor and continued, quietly.

"The truth is, we are in a Level 1 facility. That means we're peer-led and democratically run, so if we want you to stay here, and I do... then we can make it happen. I think I can convince the girls, too, but, when we meet the landlord and around the other girls, it might be best if you pretend like you are coming out of a program..."

Misty groaned. She didn't understand why housing had to come with so many conditions. It didn't make sense.

Tramaine's chest was tight and her throat was dry. She wasn't proud of asking Misty to lie, but at this point, her primary goal was avoiding having the landlord place a random stranger in her room. Misty had a job and a car and more than anything, Tramaine could tell Misty was honest--brutally honest--and that was something Tramaine could work with.

"Listen, why don't you take a shower. Freshen up and take some alone time to yourself."

Tramaine handed Misty a seafoam green towel and a little plastic baggie of personal hygiene products: a toothbrush, mini toothpaste, deodorant and some hotel soaps and shampoos. She opened the door to the bathroom and picked up a kitchen timer on the counter. She spun it to 15.

"You have 15 minutes."

It took five for the water to warm up.

Misty looked around the bathroom at the hairbrushes, towels, bottles of shampoo and other supplies in the bathroom. "Sharing a bathroom with three other women," she thought dismally.

She stepped into the hot water. Immediately she relaxed and ceased to think a thought. She dropped her head forward and let the shower stream over her.

It was the first moment she'd had to relax since she got on the bus after leaving jail. She felt a huge release. She felt like masturbating but was too tired. She needed a place to sleep. She needed to accept this offer, even if it meant not drinking or doing drugs. Even if it meant pretending like she was a recovering addict. It was time to grow up. Time to leave her bad girl ways in the dust.

She didn't even hear the buzzer of the timer as it went off. The knocks on the door shook her out of her daze and she yelled, "Just a minute," as she quickly lathered her hair and scrubbed her body.

As she dried off in the seafoam towel, she noticed her clothes were gone. She wrapped the towel around her torso and cracked open the door to the hallway.

"Honey, your times up," Joan said. "And I have irritable bowel."

"Oh, sorry. Sorry." Misty let Joan into the bathroom and stood in the hallway. She peeked into Joan and Chelsea's room, where Chelsea was still looking at her phone. "Do you know where my clothes are?"

"Oh, yeah," Chelsea responded without looking up. "We threw 'em in the laundry. Tramaine said you could wait til they're done or borrow something of hers."

Misty could hear Tramaine talking with someone in the other room.

"Tramaine?" she cautiously called out.

"Oh, Misty! You done? The landlord is here, I'd love for you to meet him!"

Tramaine walked around the corner.

"Misty, meet Gus."

Misty's jaw dropped.

Misty wanted to leave her past in the dust. But now, as she stood there in nothing but a towel, her past was staring her right in the face.

CHAPTER NINE

-

A LITTLE BACKSTORY: Misty's ex-lover got her on the FBI watch list. Her ex was writing lesbian anarchist fiction on LiveJournal.com and using real names, including Misty Cheevis. They wrote up some plot about how they and Misty were going to break into the Federal Reserve downtown and steal all the gold and give it to the homeless. The FBI took it seriously, next thing you know it's July 3rd and Misty and her lover are buying illegal fireworks across the border in Michigan and the FBI swarms in on them with helicopters and German Shepherds.

That ex... was Gus. Granted at the time Gus was Emily. But now Gus had facial hair and a rat tail and a grilled cheese in his mouth.

Misty wanted to grab him by the collar and throw him off the patio and into the dirty baby pool that was lying in the backyard. But Gus didn't have a collar. Only a grease stained wife beater and a gold chain with a scorpion charm at the end of it.

"Fuck. You." Misty said.

More back story: Once they were in jail, awaiting trial, Gus decided that the jail security had some flaws and weak points. He convinced Misty to escape with him. Well, the tunnel they dug came up three feet short of the fence and they'd have been charged with a felony if the tunnel hadn't also managed to come up three feet away from one guard peeing on another one behind a squad car. The guards agreed not to tell anyone about the attempted escape as long as Misty and Gus went back to jail and kept their mouth shut about the piss play happening in the surveillance blind spot.

"I don't know what kind of scam you're trying to pull now, but you should leave these nice old drug addicts out of it!" Misty stormed off.

"Misty?! Misty, baby! Long time no see!"

Eventually, all charges were dropped against Misty and Gus when more of Gus's writing was brought as evidence. Other stories about Misty, like the one where Misty has an orgy with wood nymphs after destroying a pipeline or the one where she gets fucked by gigantic mutant octopus tentacles while protecting the National Seed Bank corroborated Gus's claim that the bank robbery stories were strictly fiction. Additionally, an assessment of Misty's reading proved that it was impossible she had anything to do with the writing of the stories.

"Misty, you need a place to stay, girl?" Gus asked with a grin on his face. He had a gap between his two front teeth. His face was freckled and a coral flush accentuated his emerald eyes.

"Whatever you're up to, count me out! I have a Corolla that is perfectly fine to sleep in," Misty called out from behind her as she made her way up the driveway in nothing but a bath towel.

"Your grandma's Corolla is still running? Yeesh!"

"Hey! Come on, Misty. Where are you going?" Tramaine was following behind Gus.

Before she reached the street out front, Misty turned around and faced her pursuers.

"Tramaine, Gus is a scammer. You should know that. And getting into business with this one is only gonna get you in trouble, I'm speaking from experience."

Tramaine took off her sweater and put it around Misty. She led Misty back to the sober house.

"Hey, now. Come on, Misty," Gus followed behind them. "A lot has changed and I've grown a lot. I got a job! I own a house and a half!"

"And whatever tricks you pulled to make that happen, just keep it to yourself! It's better if I don't know. I'm trying to move on and I don't need anyone from my past dragging me down! Suck on that."

After borrowing a tan velour tracksuit from Tramaine, Misty

stormed down the street and back to her car. She sat there for a while, just thinking. There was a weight on her. She just wanted things to turn around. She wanted to be done with this. She wished she could be back on her air mattress, ignoring her grandma in the other room having phone sex with her elderly boyfriend. Or even at Dustin's apartment, sitting in piles of dirty clothes, screaming at noobs while playing Call of Duty online.

Instead, she was homeless. Sitting in the car where she had been sleeping for several nights.

Staring ahead out of her car, she noticed Detective Mills walk out of the tattoo shop down the way. He stopped and made some notes on his notepad before continuing into the next shop down the street.

"This asshole is actually on the case," Misty worried to herself.

She needed to focus. She had to get to the bottom of this murder before Detective Ding Dong decided to arrest Misty. Who murdered Vanessa? Bart Reyes, the gamer who worked at NubCorp had a strong alibi. Summer was still a suspect, but Misty didn't believe the extra $2.50 an hour was that strong of a motive and when Detective Mills tried to blame Misty as a suspect, Summer defended her. If Summer did it, wouldn't she just let Misty be the prime suspect?

Fucking Gus. Misty couldn't get the smell of his body odor out of her nostrils. Of all the times for her ex to show up it had to be now. The ex that got her in trouble and then humiliated her in court with graphic descriptions of her being pleasured by octopus tentacles until she squirted all over the seed of an extinct fruit which then began to sprout for the first time since the stone age.

Fucking exes, right?

"You said Vanessa had an ex," Misty confronted Summer at their next shift change.

Summer was counting cash in her office in the back. The office was small and while it wasn't untidy, it was crammed with shelving and a large cabinet for extra supplies.

"Yep, his name was Jace. He used to work with us here at Coffee

Bucket, but he quit to take a job as a barista at a fancier coffee shop and roaster in the Tremont neighborhood called 'Chevrolait.' Immediately after that, he dumped Vanessa. It was so rude and shady. Seems like he used Vanessa to get into the coffee game and then dumped her as soon as he got a better gig. And then, not long after Jace quit, Bart put in his notice. Rough."

Summer continued to do office work while Misty returned to the work iPad to do a little more research on Jace. She discovered on his social media that he hosted weekly tours of the Chevrolait coffee roasting facility, open to the public with the purchase of a 12oz bag of beans.

Misty arrived at the roastery seven minutes late. She cautiously walked into the large warehouse, where the tour had already begun.

Jace was wearing a t-shirt and blazer. He had on fitted slacks that hugged his legs. Curly blonde hair lay thick on his head and was grown out, complimenting his soft features and baby face. He was handsome, youthful and stylish.

"Organic certifications come at a high cost and require an abundance of paperwork. Also, small coffee farms that produce lower yields may use a small amount of fertilizer infrequently, which disqualifies them from organic certification, but doesn't have the disastrous impact that large corporate farms have. So the answer is, no, our beans are not certified organic and we would never require the small farms we work with to waste their time and energy for a label just so you can feel like Mother Theresa for buying it. Moving on."

Jace led the group to a roasting machine, where another employee was loading beans in. Misty noticed that all the other participants in the tour were holding bags of beans, the price of admission. She looked around and noticed a table full of bags of beans. When the employee tallying them wasn't looking, Misty swiped a bag off the table.

It was loud and busy inside the roastery, with machines whirring and buzzing and employees milling about.

"As you can see we have several machines we're working with, each one just as beautiful as the next. This here is a G47 Smithson Vintage Elite. We call her Ginny. She's our oldest roasting machine and can be a little touchy, but if you treat her right the flavor quality that she's gonna give you just won't be matched."

From the back of the tourist group, Misty made a jerking off motion. Jace led the group to another, larger machine.

"Now, this is our most state-of-the-art roasting machine. The Igneous Flame 7600. The Flame can roast up to 200 pounds of coffee at a time, but we just use one bag at a time, around 130 pounds, out of respect for the machine. Can we all take a moment of silence to respect the machine please?"

Misty had been so inspired by snatching up the bag of coffee that she had also snatched up an unopened bag of Funyuns that were sitting at what appeared to be the break table. As everyone else took a moment of silence, she cracked open the bag and chomped down on the flavorful oniony snack.

"All right everyone, that's it for my portion of the tour. If you make your way into the conference room, Juliette will lead you in a tasting of Sumatran coffees."

As the tourists made their way into the other room, they graciously thanked Jace for his time and expertise, showering him with praise like they would an oracle at a benevolent deity's temple.

Misty could tell this guy was a prick.

Sure, he was cute. He stood about 5'8" but carried himself like he was 6'3". He was cocky, too, leaning over one of the shiny roasting machines to admire himself in the reflection. He adjusted the bulge in his fitted pants. Something got him turned on. Maybe it was the compliments, maybe it was the sound of his own voice talking about the machines or maybe it was the thought that he'd gotten away with murder.

So he had a semi-hard-on. But did he have a motive? And did he have an alibi?

Misty knew how to deal with cocky guys.

"Hey, nice tour, man. You know so much about coffee, bro!" Misty approached where Jace was standing.

"Well, I've been doing this for a long time. And you need to know a lot if you want the coffee to taste right."

"Yeah, bro. And your coffee tastes the best. I've tried all the coffee shops here. Bean Zone, Mama's Cup, Coffee Bucket..." Misty paused after mentioning Jace's former employer. But he seemed like he wasn't really listening that carefully. "...You ever been to Coffee Bucket?"

"Yes. I've been to every coffee shop in Cleveland. And every roasting facility. It's actually part of my job, to scope out the competition. I don't hate what Coffee Bucket is doing. But they really don't have the scale and organization that we have here at Chev."

"Chev. Yeah, yeah. No one compares to Chev." Misty wondered why he didn't mention working at Coffee Bucket. "Did you hear about the tragedy at the Bucket?"

"I did. Yes."

"It's terrible."

"Yeah, it's a tragedy."

"Did you know her?"

"Who? What? Me? No, not personally. I didn't know her. Not well. It's such a shame. I know everyone there is devastated about it."

Wow. Wrong and wrong. What a liar.

"Well," Jace drew his fingers through his curly hair, looked Misty in the eye and smiled brightly. "I've got some roasting to do. You might want to hurry up to the cupping parlor. You don't want to miss the tasting."

Jace directed Misty to the tasting and excused himself. Misty cracked open the door to the tasting office or whatever it was called. People were sipping from small glasses and then spitting their coffee out into mugs.

"I got hints of hibiscus," one person exclaimed.

"I got some nutty notes," said another.

"Did anyone else get some pine tar flavors?"

"Ew," Misty thought. Must not be very good. She closed the door and returned to the roasting room.

People were milling about performing a variety of tasks. Roasting, bottling, labeling. She looked around for Jace, but he was nowhere in sight. She checked both bathrooms, said "hi" to the people in both, and continued to look around. But Jace was nowhere to be found.

She approached a girl with thick framed eyeglasses and a black bob haircut.

"Hey, any idea where Jace went?"

"I don't know. He stormed out of here not long after the tour ended. Peeled out in his silver 2000 Corolla. It was actually hilarious."

"Motherfucker," Misty said.

"He really is," the girl agreed.

Misty returned to her car. So the ex-boyfriend is a liar and a confirmed "motherfucker."

And he ran away like a potato bug after just a nudge of his little rock. Something was up here and Misty was going to get to the bottom of it. Shady little potato bug. Certainly one of Vanessa's friends had to know what was going on with this prick.

Misty racked her brain. Who could she ask about this guy? Who would know the real Jace? Vanessa wasn't close to her coworker Summer, but there was someone else she was close to, wasn't there?

For some reason every time she thought back to the shop all she saw were the lady's huge jugs who had led her to NubCorp Industries. She kept trying to think about who else had come in the shop that knew Vanessa. She mostly kept on seeing enormous breasts. Had to be double D's. Double D's... that rang a bell. Double D. D&D.

The mysterious girl in the hoodie! Vanessa's friend from Dungeons and Dragons came in on Misty's first day of work. Misty smiled. Her list of suspects was growing.

CHAPTER TEN

-

MISTY SPENT THE NEXT FEW DAYS anxiously trying to figure out her next move. There were no more tours scheduled at the Chevrolait roasting facility, so Misty had no good excuse to stalk Jace. Other than him, her only unexplored lead was the person in the hoodie who claimed to play Dungeons and Dragons with Vanessa.

Summer had no idea who they were either.

"Honestly, I wouldn't even know them if they walked in right now--their hood was pulled so low I barely got a glimpse of who was underneath it."

It was true. Misty didn't get much of a look at who the person was either that night. It was her first day working and everything was such a blur as it was.

A few days later at work, Misty was making drinks while the AA meeting was going on in the other room.

"SHIT!" Misty screamed, causing the AA meeting to come to a grinding halt.

Misty had spilled a gallon of milk all over herself, dousing her shirt.

"Damn it! This was my last clean shirt!" Misty shouted.

Tramaine rushed out of the shop and returned a few minutes later with some fresh clothes for Misty.

"Thanks, Tramaine, I owe you," Misty looked at the clothes. They didn't seem like anything the impeccable Tramaine would wear. "Hah! I didn't think you even owned jeans."

"They're just for when I have to run out late or something," Tramaine said, rolling her eyes.

Misty took the clothes to the bathroom. She pulled on the frayed jeans and hoodie and looked at herself in the mirror. Staring back at her was the person from the D&D group.

"I don't know, Misty," Tramaine hesitated when Misty confronted her after the AA meeting. "Yeah, it was me. I did D&D with Vanessa, but I don't know if I want to go back this week."

"Why?" Misty asked.

"Just because!" Tramaine replied. "It's... it's just too much!"

Now, Misty was aggravated. "What do you know, Tramaine. Do you know something about the murder?"

"No... no. I mean, I don't think I do..." Tramaine looked at her feet.

"Then you'll take me to the next meeting," Misty said.

Tramaine wanted to know why Misty was so curious about Vanessa.

"I have my reasons," Misty said. "I won't bother you about why you're being so weird if you won't bother me about why I'm being weird. Deal?"

Tramaine thought about it. She was hesitant to return to Dungeons and Dragons that week. Hesitant. But she also had reasons compelling her to return--unfinished business. She thought about it for a few minutes while Misty helped some customers. When she was finished Tramaine spoke up.

"Fine. I can take you," she said. "But, there's a catch..."

"What's the catch?" Misty was stirring a pitcher of iced tea. Misty was no stranger to 'a catch.' "Whips? Chains? If I'm going to end up in a leather swing just make sure it's really secured into the ceiling."

"No, no. Nothing like that, Misty. It's kind of stupid, really, but it's the rules that we agreed to when we joined the game," Tramaine stirred her coffee with a wooden stirrer, for no reason really, considering she hadn't put any cream or sugar into it. "We have a rule that once we walk into D&D, we have to be in character. We won't be responded to if we go out of character and if we get out of character more than twice, we will be removed from the game and our character will die in a boring accident."

"Fine. I don't know what any of that means, but I'm game."

Tramaine looked at Misty, who poured herself some of the iced tea, took a sip, gagged and spit it out in the sink.

"Blech. Just right." She placed the pitcher into the refrigerator.

"Do you know what D&D is, Misty?"

"I don't know, exactly, but I've been brainstorming. My first guess is Dykes and Domination."

"What? No!"

"Sorry, you don't look dykey, but you do look like you could be a dominatrix. I hope it doesn't stand for Daddies and Domination."

"Eew! Misty! D&D stands for Dungeons and Dragons!"

"Okay, so I'm half right. I get Dungeons, but what's Dragons? Is that another gay subgroup like bears or otters?"

"Misty, it isn't a sex thing! It's a fantasy role playing game from the '70s. It's for kids and families... it's basically make-believe with some rules."

Misty was confused, but she'd had some familiarity with role playing. Gus used to like it when Misty pretended she was a whore in a Wild West brothel and he was a nasty cowboy. Tramaine continued to explain.

"Each player has a role--a character. The character has a defined set of skills and abilities they can use throughout the adventure, like in a video game. They also have a level of health that can be depleted, resulting in their death."

Tramaine's eyes lost focus as she stared off into a distant world, the real world, where death meant that someone was gone forever. She took a deep breath and continued.

"The Dungeon Master, or DM, facilitates the characters as they pursue their quest. The DM plays all the other roles, including enemies and allies. They also have maps of the dungeons or forests or castles where the characters are roaming."

Misty nodded, though she wasn't really following along. First of all she could still taste the white peach tea on her tongue and she was wondering why anyone would ever drink unsweetened iced tea. Second, Misty didn't really care what D&D was. She was gonna go no matter what it was. She needed more information about Vanessa and if that meant pretending to crawl in a dungeon or whatever, then... whatever!

While Misty was closing the shop, Tramaine went home to pick up her bag of dice and her D&D binder, which contained all her character information. As Misty locked up, Tramaine returned to the front of the shop.

"Here," she handed Misty a notebook. "You can use this to write down information for your character. Have you decided on one yet?"

"I have one in mind," Misty lied.

Tramaine sat in the passenger seat and navigated while Misty drove to the house where they'd be playing the game.

The game was being hosted by Theo, the Dungeon Master. He lived in a carriage house in Horsetown, a little peninsula of a neighborhood bordered by an industrial spring factory to the east, railroad tracks to the south and an electric power grid to the west. It was home to horses and stables before being turned into housing in the 1930s. The only way in or out was to the north.

Theo was a large black man, with an abundance of hair on his head and face. This wasn't his first game of D&D. In fact, he was a D&D legend, hosting many games amongst friends and strangers for money. He demanded total immersion in the fantasy. From the moment one entered the room, they were expected to embody their role and leave their own personality outside. Participants never spoke to Theo outside of the game, except through scheduling emails.

He was strict, but he was the best.

Tramaine's role was "Snake," a half-elf ranger spy. A beast-master, she could calm and pacify even the most heinous of monsters and spoke the language of beasts. Her bond with creatures caused her to feel like part of the herd, making her extremely loyal and protective of her crew. But turn on her and she would be vicious as her namesake.

"Remind you of anyone?" Tramaine asked.

"Uh..." Misty racked her brain.

"She's like me," Tramaine said.

The neighborhood was dimly lit by sparse orange streetlights. Misty parked on the street under a large Catalpa and they made their way down the driveway past the front house. It reminded Misty of the sober house she was thinking about living in before she realized Gus was running the stupid thing. She felt a rage bubble up inside her gut. She was interrupted by Tramaine, who pointed out a tall lanky person waiting outside the front door of the rear house, under an awning.

"That's David. He's a security guard at Target, but in the game he plays Mokograk, a half-orc paladin raised by chicken-worshiping nuns. He's righteous, powerful and sensitive."

Also waiting outside the front door was a person in a tank-top and biking shorts with striking natural red hair. "That's Nico, an administrator for a housing non-profit. In the game they play Wart, a sheltered hill-dwarf mage that knows all you can know about healing potions from their hill, but outside of their home environment they're clueless."

Misty peered down the driveway at the two people waiting casually in front of the back house. If Tramaine's role was like her real life personality, maybe the others were also like their fantasy roles in real life. She could picture it. Maybe David was powerful and sensitive with strong moral beliefs due to his Unitarian upbringing. And maybe Nico grew up sheltered and comfortable on a farm outside Toledo before being kicked out for being queer, forced to move to Cleveland, where they felt lost and unfamiliar.

"What was Vanessa's role?" Misty inquired.

"Vanessa was Doreena, a powerful, yet mysterious sorceress with a dark past, teetering between saving the world and enacting gruesome revenge upon its wrongdoers."

"Great. Mysterious with a dark past, huh? That helps a lot," Misty thought to herself.

"What's your character? My character will introduce yours as my guest when we enter the dungeon," Tramaine asked.

"How about Linda... a stay-at-home mom."

Tramaine rolled her eyes and let off a slight giggle.

"Hey everyone. I'm glad we're meeting. How are you guys doing?"

The reunion was somber. It had been one week since they'd last met, when Vanessa hadn't shown up.

"I'm glad we're meeting, too. It would be weird to take the week off and then come back," said Nico. "Besides, Theo thought it was important that we meet, to get some closure on losing one of our group."

Tramaine nodded. "This is Misty, she's gonna sit in with us tonight as my guest. I cleared it with Theo."

"Replacing Vanessa already?" asked David, looking down at Misty from his looming height of six foot two.

"I'm not replacing Vanessa," Tramaine snapped. "Misty is just joining us this week. She was Vanessa's friend and she wanted to experience one of Vanessa's pastimes."

Tramaine's swift little lie didn't go unnoticed by Misty. Tramaine didn't know Misty's reason for wanting to be there and it was generous for her to provide Misty with some cover. But why? She looked innocent, but Tramaine was also cunning.

"Hi, I'm Nico. But you should get used to calling me Wart." Nico didn't offer a hand to shake or anything, and in fact just kind of took a step backwards.

"Let's go."

The front door opened into a candle-lit room, with a roaring fireplace. A large, circular wooden table sat in the middle of the room, surrounded by large, straight backed wooden chairs. Mystical, Irish-pub pan-flute new-age sounding music played softly from a Bose Bluetooth speaker on a bookshelf along one of the walls. A water cooler glowed in the corner.

"No couch," Misty thought. "So maybe it isn't a sex club. But they do know how to set a mood."

She couldn't tell if she was feeling horny or just angry at having been reminded of Gus and the homes he owned and rented to drug addicts, the rotten scammer.

Suddenly the music switched and a looming sitar started playing. From out of the Bose speaker came a voice:

"When we last left off, our heroes were disturbed by the disappearance of one of their own. Putting a wrench in their search for the Lost Dragon's Treasure, the crew was stuck in a dark cave, surrounded by giant spiders, reanimated skeleton dwarves and poisonous fungi. Having just defeated a spider queen, a new tunnel is revealed. This is The Quest of the Dragon's Treasure..." The music began to pick up speed and intensity. "And I am your dungeon master!"

Misty hadn't noticed the fog emanating from the doorframe leading to the kitchen, but when the strobe light started flashing in her peripheral vision, her attention was redirected. Out from the fog rolled Theo in a wheelchair, with a box of supplies on his lap.

He made his way to the table and set up his supplies, finishing just as the music died down.

"Roll for perception," he stated, bruskly.

The participants all grabbed their twenty-sided die and rolled. Misty looked on, confused. Tramaine grabbed some pink dice with blue dots out of her bag and slid them to Misty. The dice were all different shapes. Tramaine picked up the twenty-sided one and handed it to Misty, giving her a glance that urged her to roll.

"10"

"4"

"15"

"9"

"Snake hears a shuffling sound coming from the room behind them."

"I ready my bow and turn to look at what's coming," Tramaine/Snake replied.

"From around the corner enters a strange being," Theo said, motioning toward Misty.

"Linda!" Snake shouted, gleefully. "It's my friend Linda, whom I summoned using my crystal shard." Tramaine crossed a line through the words "crystal shard" in the inventory column of her character sheet.

David spoke up as Mokograk, "Aha, I see the beastmaster hath brought with her another beast. Does the beast speak the common tongue?"

Misty shot a glare at David. "No, but I do recognize bitch speak when I hear it. Beast? How about you come close enough to hear how my fists sound when they do the talking, huh?"

Misty hit her palm loudly. "You hear that? What's it saying to you? Bitch. Bitch. Bitch. That's what I'm hearing."

"Whoa, whoa, whoa. We're here in peace. I offer the beast a pallet of Vedushian calming salve."

"Who are you calling douch-ey?" Misty asked, turning to Nico/Wart.

Tramaine had a grin on her face. "This is Linda. She's not a beast. She's a human warrior and a stay-at-home mom."

The group looked perplexed.

"And what business hath you in breeching the Dragon's lair?" Asked Mokograk. "I am here to protect the monastery where I was raised from plundering and violence by the Dragon beast whose appetite for destruction hath no end."

"I am here to recover the great mortar of Dothendrell, a powerful artifact, stolen from our peaceful enclave in Dothendrell Hill," added Wart.

"And I am contracted to provide intel and protection and reap my rewards from the lair's treasure," said Snake.

"That dragon put a dent in my minivan..." Misty said. The group was skeptical. Theo furrowed his brow and looked at Tramaine, who bit her lip and pretended like she didn't notice.

"Minivan?" Wart muttered.

"A gypsy..." Mokograk whispered suspiciously.

"...and it scared my children." Misty added. "And no one scares my children and gets away with it."

Misty pulled that one out of nowhere. It excited her, playing the role that her family always expected her to play. The one her aunts and cousins had played with ease. For some people, fantasy meant having a tail or shooting acid from their hands. But Misty shooting acid was already a reality, and she stopped doing that a few years ago. For her, there was nothing more fantasy than being a well-adjusted mother of four, devoted wife and strong powerful member of the community. Sometimes Misty felt like that actually was what she wanted, to feel secure with a husband and a home and kids playing street hockey in the cul-de-sac. But was that also a fantasy? Would she feel secure or would she feel stuck, living at a dead end.

"I loot the spider queen's corpse," Snake said, continuing with the game.

"You find 3 potions," Theo noted.

"Gimme one of those." Misty nudged Snake. "What's it do?"

"Heals you for ten hit points."

"Does it give you a buzz?"

"Moving on," Theo's voice boomed. "As you enter the room that was being guarded by the spider queen, it's damp and cold and dimly lit by some bioluminescent moss."

"Roll for identification," Wart said. "18."

"The moss is harmless, Delicatia Moglipherus," Theo announced.

"I'll collect some, it has healing properties."

"As Wart walks to the wall of the cavern room, he steps in something wet and sticky."

"Roll for identification..."

"It's blood."

The mood grew somber.

"On the ground, in the corner lies a dark mass. On closer inspection, it cannot be denied that this is the body of your previous companion, Doreena."

"Doreena. No," Snake gasped. "I move to the body and check for a pulse."

"No pulse."

"She's dead," Snake told the other members of the party.

"The spider must have dragged her here, to save for later."

"Doreena would never have been killed by a mere spider. She was too powerful," Wart countered. "I suspect foul play."

"Are you suggesting that one of us murdered her? By my Gods I reject the accusation and warn you that such accusations do not come without consequence!" Mokograk shouted.

"I think he's suggesting I'm responsible," Snake admitted.

The room grew somber. A crash of thunder was heard from outside and it began to rain.

"I want to know more about this wench," Misty said, throwing in a word she'd heard used before that she felt fit in with the language the group was using.

"She wasn't a wench, Linda," Snake explained. "She was a warlock."

"Wench, warlock. Whatever. Who was she hanging out with? We need to know so that we can make sure they're not coming after us, too."

"I did not know the wench..." Wart stated.

Tramaine rolled her eyes. "When did we decide she was a wench? Can we show a little respect, please?"

"But I'd heard some rumors that she was involved in some suspect activity?"

"Really?! What did you hear? Where did you hear it?" Linda sounded a lot like Misty.

Nico's eyes darted to the Dungeon Master and then back to the table.

"I... I can't say for sure..."

"Just then three undead skeletons enter the room!" Theo boomed. Roll for initiative.

The group defeated the skeletons, however while everyone else was fighting Linda tried to loot Doreena's dead body for clues. Just then, a blaze of fire burst into the room from the far door.

"The dragon!" Snake announced.

The group proceeded into the next room in the dungeon, a giant cavern with a large treasure being protected by an angry and powerful dragon.

"Wait, I need to know more about Doreena! Were there any clues on her body?" Misty demanded.

The rest of the party focused on defeating the dragon, infuriating Misty.

"I attack the dragon with my longsword," said Mokograk.

"I douse the team in fireproof oil," announced Wart.

"I shoot the dragon with my longbow, aiming for its eyes," said Snake.

"I throw my potion at the dragon," said Linda, not knowing what weapons she was even working with.

"The dragon is healed by 10 HP," Theo responded.

"What the heck!" Mokograk screamed.

"Whatever, I'm on the dragon's side until someone tells me what's going on with Vanessa! I mean Doreena!"

Misty and the dragon attacked the team until Wart fainted and was lying on the ground. Mokograk was deciding whether or not he wanted to use his last turn to revive Wart or attack the dragon. Snake was hiding in another room and Linda, having somehow rolled three consecutive 20's, was now riding the dragon's back.

Theo was furious. Never had anyone sabotaged his story like this before. Somehow, Misty's luck with the dice was allowing her to control the entire game. Every attempt Theo made to reign power back in was countered by some hairbrained idea from Misty.

"We surrender!" yelled Mokograk. "We'll tell you everything you need to know!"

Theo slammed his hands on the table. "TIME!"

Everyone looked up.

"Time is up. That ends today's session. We will resume next week."

He wheeled himself out of the room.

Outside, everyone was exhausted and angry.

"What the heck! I still don't know anything more about Vanessa!" Misty said to Tramaine. "I thought someone here knew something, Tramaine!"

"I think someone does! I just thought we'd be able to get it out of him during the session, but apparently it wasn't going to work out that way."

"Thanks a lot, Misty. Thanks to you, Wart is dead!" David was legitimately angry.

"It's okay, I was kind of getting sick of Wart, anyway. Now I can make a new character. I'm thinking a princess or something." Nico didn't seem all that phased. "I actually thought that was a pretty fun session. You had some creative ideas, Misty. I didn't expect you to floss the dragon's teeth in order to strengthen your bond with it, but it worked."

Just then the front door squeaked open and out came Theo. Tramaine was shocked; no one had ever seen Theo outside of the game before.

"You ruined our game," he said to Misty. "We had been on that campaign for almost a year."

"Sorry, man," she said. "I'm just trying to figure out what happened with Vanessa."

"I've thought about it. It's been a long time since I've seen someone play D&D with your enthusiasm and creativity. And recklessness. You had no respect for my authority and no respect for the game."

"Ugh, whatever, dude."

"But you stayed in character. Linda is a powerful woman. They say that the first character you make in D&D is the most like yourself."

"Thanks, but I modeled her after my grandma and aunts. I'm nothing like them."

"I met Vanessa at a meeting of a group of local anarchists. I grew to like her and invited her to join the D&D group. I stopped attending the anarchist meetings because I simply lost interest. To be honest, their efforts seemed more fantasy to me than potions and dragons. But as far as I know, Vanessa continued with the group. I can't tell you exactly what they were involved in, but I can tell you when and where they meet," Theo wrote some information down in his D&D notebook and ripped the paper out. He folded it and handed it to Misty.

"Linda is more than welcome back at Dungeons and Dragons, if you choose."

"We'll see," Misty said. "And thank you." She held up the paper and nodded at Theo as he went back in the house.

The group dispersed and Misty drove Tramaine home.

"I don't know why you're so interested in finding out who killed Vanessa..." Tramaine said, breaking the silence.

Misty didn't want to explain to Tramaine how she'd been in the wrong place at the wrong time, so she remained silent.

But... I miss Vanessa, too," Tramaine continued. "So I hope you figure it out."

"Why didn't you want to go back to D&D? It seemed like you were having fun."

Tramaine's voice dropped low.

"Two weeks ago, during our Dungeons and Dragons game, I attempted to deal a fatal blow to an enemy, but I rolled a one. I accidentally stabbed Vanessa's character, instead. One week later, Vanessa didn't show up to D&D and I thought it was because of me. I was in a dark place. When I visited the coffee shop to apologize, I found out Vanessa was dead. In a way I feel somehow responsible. I know it doesn't make sense. But I think if we were to find her real killer, I'd maybe feel less guilt. At least, I hope I would."

Misty was confused. She didn't understand how someone could feel guilt or responsibility for someone dying just because they had also died in a fantasy game. It was kind of a silly way to think. Then again, those D&D people were all pretty silly and they had vivid imaginations, so maybe it made sense to them somehow.

After dropping Tramaine off at her house, she thought about Linda. Theo said people were most like the first character they made.

Unlike Linda, Misty wasn't a stay at home mom, living in a cul-de-sac, protecting her kids. But Misty was powerful and she was protective. She was protecting herself from being wrongfully convicted of a crime. And she was protecting her community from whoever this killer was who was on the loose.

It was time for Misty to be on the aggressive, like Linda. It was time for Misty to find this murderer, even if it meant breaking a few rules and making a few people mad.

The night when she stumbled upon Vanessa's dead body, Misty wasn't in the wrong place at the wrong time. The killer was.

CHAPTER ELEVEN

-

The next morning at Coffee Bucket, Misty's eyes were rolling up in her head as she poured almost eight ounces of milk directly on the counter, completely missing the steaming pitcher.

"Misty..." Summer said as she elegantly grabbed the bottle of milk from Misty's hands while simultaneously sopping milk off the counter with a rag.

Tramaine sat at the counter nursing a black coffee. "Honey," she said. "You need a good night's rest. The room's still open and it won't be for long. Just come stay with us."

"I can sleep in the Corolla," Misty muttered.

"Can you?" Summer asked. She was dressed like a French mime and had on an excessive amount of eyeliner. "Misty, this job isn't hard, but, like, you at least need to be awake for it. Also, I'm trying not to talk today, so..." She zipped her mouth shut with her finger, mimed locking it and then opened her mouth again to swallow the imaginary key.

"I'll find a place to stay," Misty said through a yawn.

Misty was tired. She knew she needed a rest, but her brain wouldn't stop working, trying to put the pieces of this puzzle together. Every time she thought she was getting a step closer, things seemed to get more complicated. At this point anyone could have done it. Hell, she didn't particularly feel good about the people she met at the D&D game. Any one of them had the potential to snap and mistake reality for fantasy.

She was up all night trying to piece it together. Like Doreena, her character in D&D, Vanessa was mysterious and had only grown more so with each bit of information Misty had squeezed out of people. First, it seemed like everyone agreed that Vanessa was a bit uptight and stressed out. Then there was the fact that her ex-boyfriend Jace had dumped her after moving on to a better job in the coffee industry. On top of that, Jace was avoiding questions. Misty certainly wasn't done with Jace. Now, there was this secretive anarchist meeting group to deal with.

"Misty!"

She was standing in front of a puddle of iced tea as she kept pouring in an already full glass.

"Girl," Tramaine grabbed some napkins from the dispenser. "At least come to the house tonight for dinner. We're making stuffed cabbage and doing a puzzle. A home-cooked meal might be good for you."

"Cabbage? I don't think so." Misty winced. "Y'all never heard of ordering a pizza? Besides, I have to go to an antichrist book club meeting tonight."

Summer and Tramaine looked at each other.

"Antichrist book club meeting?" Summer asked.

"Yah..." Misty said. "It's top secret."

"Okay, whatever you do in your free time is up to you. Just try to get home... or in your car or whatever and get some sleep afterward, Misty. We're running low on dry towels, so I'm really gonna need you to be able to pour liquids into their containers properly until the fresh ones get delivered next week."

"What even is an antichrist?" Misty asked Tramaine after work.

"Antichrist? Misty it's an anarchist meeting, not an antichrist meeting."

"Oh... I guess I was just picturing the worst. But I don't know what an anarchist is either. I think Gus was one at one point, so whatever it is, I'm sure it isn't good."

"To be honest, I'm not super familiar with it either. I looked it up and from what I found online, it looks pretty scary. I looked at the images for like a minute before I got scared the government was going to come get me. From what I gather, they believe in having no form of government and like, no laws and stuff. They love to break windows of businesses and set police cars on fire from what I understand. I think they're into punk music and they might be vegans. Honestly, I'm not totally sure. I'm a little nervous about this meeting."

Theo's book club contact had emailed Tramaine an article about anarchism that they would be discussing at the meeting, which Tramaine had shared with Misty.

"Did you read the article?" Tramaine asked.

"Yeah, couldn't put it down." Misty said, sarcastically. "I loved it so much I read it twice."

The meeting was held at a warehouse on the east side, in the undeveloped former industrial zone between Downtown and the Cleveland Clinic campus. Misty and Tramaine agreed that they needed to dress the part, to try to fit in with the anarchists. Tramaine let Misty borrow some clothes. They were somewhat matching in a black and red color scheme.

It was a "leaderless group;" however, the warehouse happened to be owned by Cleveland Aquaponics, a green company that made aquaponics systems. The company was founded by Grover, the inventor of a novel and efficient aquaponics system along with his friend Michelle, an investor who worked in private equity. They ran it together with Big Ben, an environmentalist. The business was incredibly successful and the young founders were even featured in an article in The New York Times.

They were well known and respected by a certain progressive crowd in Cleveland and though the anarchist book club was leaderless, it was hard for attendees to keep their attention off the hosts, all of whom were quite attractive and charismatic.

There were enough people in attendance at the meeting for Misty and Tramaine to slip in and sit down on the pillows on the floor without being noticed, however both noticed that they were the only ones dressed in what they had deemed to be anarchist garb. The rest of the attendees looked more like they belonged in a library than at a rebellious gathering. The meeting hadn't started, yet, so people were still milling about socializing.

Eventually, Grover walked out of a room in the center of the large warehouse, followed behind by Michelle and Big Ben. They sat on the pillows and the rest of the attendees formed a large, scattered circle around the space.

"Welcome, everyone! I hope everyone had a great week!" Grover announced, jovially. He wore skinny jeans and combat boots and a black tanktop that contrasted pale, white skin. He had long black hair, divided into two tight pigtails that went down to his shoulders. His green eyes were all the more striking in contrast to the bushy beard that concealed the rest of his face, but it was obvious that underneath all the hair was a charming smile.

"I hope everyone enjoyed the reading," Michelle added. Michelle was tall and elegant. She wore a vintage skirt, Stella McCartney sweater and Chanel flats. Bangles adorned her wrists and her hair was natural, curly and strikingly complimentary of her round face and radiant, obsidian hue.

"I'll start, if you don't mind," Grover declared. "I'm sure some of you may be wondering why we chose a reading about the lives of mushrooms and other fungi."

The room filled with giggles and nods.

"Well," Grover continued, "In addition to being about one of our favorite topics--plants--it also offers an example of anarchy in the natural world."

"Exactly," Michelle took up the discussion. "What really spoke to me was how decentralized these huge, powerful and successful networks were. There could be miles of mycelia in just one handful of healthy soil, all communicating with each other, making decisions without a real center! Yet we still function and operate with a highly centralized government that very often makes decisions that threaten the livelihood of our own species."

The group nodded in agreement and cooed and awed at Michelle's eloquent observation.

"I love that, Michelle," Grover shook his head. "Beautifully put. For me, I was drawn to just how small and insignificant we are as humans. We like to think that we are so powerful and mighty, and certainly in terms of the damage human industrialization has done, one wouldn't be entirely wrong to think we are powerful. However, everywhere humans have done damage, fungi seem to return: Chernobyl, Hiroshima, Cleveland."

Everyone laughed.

Big Ben, who was off to the side. Though he lounged in the seat of a skid steer with his bare feet over the steering wheel, he was noticeably large: certainly over six-feet tall and his body filled out the overalls he was wearing. His walnut hair was curly and covered most of his rusty bronze body. He shared his two-cents.

"It's because fungi acquire nutrients by secreting digestive enzymes into the environment allowing them to digest basically anything. In my composting work, to me, it's the digestion that is most empowering. Death is life."

The group hummed in agreement and contemplation. It was heavy, but it made you think.

Misty was nodding off and let out a loud snort. Tramaine nudged her.

"Misty, wake up!"

"I thought these people broke windows and set cars on fire."

"Well, I guess it's more philosophical than we realized."

"It's boring as hell. It's like a bible study..."

Indeed, the discussion had turned to the interconnectedness of mycorrhizal networks.

"The trees are linked by a network of fungi underground, allowing the trees to communicate with each other as one giant organism. It's all connected. Indeed we, too, are connected with the fungi as the spores float through the air and connect with our bodies."

The group was stunned and in awe, as Grover began to unbraid his own hair.

"The fungal network is reminiscent of Mother Nature's hands, flowing through all of natural life just as the veins flow and circulate life through our own bodies. The network is speaking to us all, if we're only willing to listen to Mother Nature speak."

People in the room began to actually clap after this expression of oneness with nature.

Misty was feeling antsy. She couldn't just sit here and listen to everyone coo over everything Grover said. There had to be something better she could do. She looked around the room and found a clock on the wall above one of the aquaponics prototypes. It was almost seven. She knew Chevrolait closed at 8 o'clock. She still had time to see if Jace was working. Maybe she could press him one more time about his relationship with Vanessa.

"Hey, let's get out of here," she poked at Tramaine.

Tramaine was listening intently to the discussion.

"I think I'm gonna stay here," Tramaine said. " I'm gonna ask around afterwards and see if anyone knows anything about Vanessa. I can call a cab to take me home."

Misty didn't want to stay for another second. She was bored out of her mind. She grabbed the gas mask she'd borrowed from Gus to bring to the discussion and hurried out of the warehouse through the open garage door.

In her car she headed towards Chevrolait, in Tremont. She felt her stomach knot up. She couldn't deny the discomfort. She was stalking Jace. She knew he was scheduled to be working that day because she'd called the shop pretending to be from the roasting facility and another employee gave her his full schedule for the week. Idiot.

It was sensitive territory, considering she'd already gone to jail for stalking her old boss at Pizza Fever. But Misty was a tiger and she was hungry. She needed some real information, something substantial that would lead her to Vanessa's killer. This wasn't just some freak murder in an alley. There were no fingerprints on the murder weapon and they didn't even rob the store--they were there for one reason: murder. Someone knew Vanessa would be working. They knew she'd be taking out the trash back there and they wanted her dead. But who?

Jace was her ex-boyfriend. Based on that information alone he was a likely suspect. Even if he didn't do it, he had to know something. He had to have some important information on what Vanessa was up to and who she was involved with. Maybe he knew about her involvement with the anarchists. Misty needed something to chew on, something that would get her closer to the answer.

The cafe was on a slow and shady street with parking on both sides. It was an elegant cafe in a building with an old facade, adorned by columns and buttresses and decorative ledges. Large windows revealed a classy interior with refined simplicity and detail.

She parked her car directly in front of the cafe and got out. The cafe was just as beautiful inside as it was on the outside: sparkling fixtures cascaded from the tin-tiled ceilings, granite countertops were adorned with complex coffee brewing systems and machines, magnificent and colorful delicacies glowed within the sparkling clean pastry case and classy patrons were perched comfortably on comfortable and soft upholstered furniture.

Jace was kneeling behind the counter, cleaning out a cabinet. He had a fat ass for a white boy, Misty noticed as he squatted down to reach into the back of the cabinet, the ties of his apron resting on his juicy shelf. It seemed like he was always wearing the tightest pants, but with a caboose like that maybe it wasn't easy finding the right fit.

"I'll be with you in just a second," he said as he got up, with his pants sucked in between his ass cheeks like they were vacuum sealed. He washed his hands in the sink and turned toward the register. As soon as he saw Misty, his eyes shifted with recognition.

"Hi! What can we get for you, today, my friend?" he asked, trying hard to be nonchalant.

Misty wasn't thirsty. Well, after watching Jace stand up she was kind of thirsty. But mostly she was hungry. Hungry for some answers. She felt like Linda in the Dungeon. She didn't have time to play games anymore. She didn't have time to let Jace slip away, again. She was a powerful dragon mama and she needed to protect herself from having this murder pinned on her.

"I'll take a chocolate milk. Cold," she said.

Jace was perplexed by the order. He didn't usually encounter grown adults ordering chocolate milk. He recognized her from the Roastery. She was that weirdo that asked him about Vanessa.

Misty stood at the counter as he poured her a glass of milk. She tapped her fingers on the counter.

"Do I know you from somewhere? You look familiar," Jace said.

"I know you dated Vanessa," Misty said.

"Everybody knows that," Jace responded.

"Then maybe you'll know what she was doing with those antichrists."

"What?"

"Anarchists, sorry. What was Vanessa getting up to over there with Johnny Appleseed?"

"Sorry, I don't know what you're talking about."

"Why? Were you involved, too?"

"No way! I was not involved!" Jace shot Misty a look.

"So she was up to something!" Jace's reaction made it clear.

"Listen, I don't have any idea what you're getting at, but you have your milk and you can either go have a seat in the cafe or you can leave. I have to go do inventory in the back."

Jace went to the back and another barista came to the front to take his spot. Misty took a seat at a small table near the front window.

Misty was shaking. She was closer than she realized. Vanessa was up to something--something that Jace wanted to remain as unconnected with as possible. Misty couldn't stop bouncing her leg underneath the table. She contemplated just rushing to the back room to find out more information, but she couldn't do anything illegal or anything that would draw unsavory attention.

Misty took a chug of her chocolate milk.

"Damn. This shit is good!" She said, a chocolate mustache glimmering on her upper lip.

"It's farm fresh from a local dairy," the barista piped in from the counter.

Misty gave him a disgusted look. "Who asked?" she shouted.

Misty looked out the window. It was dusk and the neighborhood glowed. Tall trees shaded the street as a woman pushed a stroller down the sidewalk, waving as she passed an old couple who sat on their front porch. Misty wondered if there were any places for rent in the area. It seemed like a nice place to live. She watched as a bicycle rolled out onto the street from next to the coffee shop.

"He could get it," Misty thought. As she put her face closer to the window pane to get a closer look she recognized the booty bouncing up and down as the cyclist pedaled away. "Jace!"

Misty slammed the last of her milk and bursted out the front door. "Get your ass back here!" she yelled down the street, disturbing the elderly couple and concerned mother.

Misty opened the door to her Corolla and got in, but when she tried to start the car, the engine didn't even make a rattle. She put her foot on the break and kept turning the key, but the car wouldn't start.

"What the fuck?" she shouted, slamming her hand on the steering wheel violently like a psychopath.

She got out of the car to look under the hood and as she did, she noticed that the back tire had also been slashed.

"Motherfucker!" she screamed loudly, holding out the last syllable for an irregularly long amount of time. She took a breath and looked around. The elderly man looked at her over his shoulder as he ushered his wife inside. She decided to leave before the cops got called on her. She hustled down the street as fast as she could, holding her pants up with one hand.

At dusk the aquaponics warehouse had seemed cozy and romantic, but as the sun went down and everything grew dark, only a few lights came on in the building and Tramaine was worried that maybe she'd stayed too long. She had been trying to gather information about Vanessa, asking other book club attendees if they'd known her. She didn't find out many details, but Vanessa definitely had been a regular at the meetings and she was apparently pretty outspoken.

One person Tramaine spoke with said that she often argued with and criticized "The Big Three" for not having a radical enough approach. Another said that one week Vanessa had suggested a reading about "Direct Action," claiming that anything else was a waste of time. People said she was smart and passionate but combative and easily frustrated.

Tramaine didn't want to lose any of what she'd heard, so she had found her way to the restroom in order to jot down notes in her D&D notebook. The restroom was large and cold, with tiled walls and damp floors. Stalls lined one wall and sinks lined the other with translucent windows hugging the ceiling. It was illuminated by fluorescent tubes that hung from the ceiling, some of which had burnt out.

By the time Tramaine left the bathroom, it seemed as though everyone had cleared out of the facility. She noticed the garage door had been closed and as she looked for another exit, she heard some voices coming from the other side of the large room, behind a living wall of ferns and other tropical plants. She put her phone away and snuck closer. A light was glowing on the concrete floor from behind the wall, likely coming out of a window. She chose to sneak around the other side of the wall to get a better look.

Behind the wall was an enclosed meeting room, with a conference table. Tramaine could see Grover, Big Ben and Michelle around the table. Michelle and Big Ben were sitting, but Grover was pacing back and forth, agitated, waving his hands as he spoke. The words were muffled through the walls, but Tramaine could tell they were arguing as sound wafted above the walls. There wasn't a ceiling on the room. It had been built there in the middle of the warehouse, with just walls and a door to partition it off. If she could get to the top of the living wall, she could probably hear what they were saying.

The wall had little terraces and bowls jutting out from it for plants to grow in. Tramaine tested their strength, putting her foot up on one of the platforms. She didn't have a lot of experience rock climbing, but she had always been an agile kid, climbing trees and fences.

The wall made a creak as she put her full weight on one of the narrow platforms, crushing a few leaves underneath her foot. She paused to make sure no one had heard anything. The muffled arguing continued. Slowly, Tramaine crawled her way to the top of the wall and peered over, between the leaves of a fern, on the meeting below.

"That was boring as hell. It felt like a bible study," Big Ben said, with his dirty bare feet up on the table.

"Who cares if it was boring!" Grover replied, clearly annoyed. "Did you even recognize half the people out there? Guaranteed there were undercover cops out there. What were we supposed to talk about? Police abolition? We're fucked!"

"You don't know that--there could be cops here any week. If we really care about that we could have just cancelled this week's meeting," Michelle responded.

"Oh, like that wouldn't have been suspicious. Cancel the meeting one week after one of its most controversial members is killed!" Grover plopped down in a chair and put his head in his hands. "At some point someone's going to find out what we did."

"So what? We're making a difference. Not everything is black and white, cut and dry. Sometimes you have to do what you have to do. The earth is a system of constant death and regeneration," Big Ben's gaze drifted off and up and if he hadn't been daydreaming about the lifecycle of organisms in soil, he would have seen Tramaine drop her head below the wall.

Tramaine's heart had already been pounding, but now she could tell her breathing was speeding up and almost becoming audible.

"We made that choice and we have to live with it," she heard Michelle say as she started back down the wall.

The garage door had been shut, but Tramaine found an exit sign glowing on the far wall of the warehouse. Barefoot, she ran as fast as she could without making noise, to the door, glancing behind her every couple steps. The door made a loud creak as she exited, but she didn't look back, sprinting down an alley, where she hid behind a dumpster for thirty minutes before walking another six blocks to a convenience store that called her a cab.

By the time Misty found herself sneaking down Gus's driveway to the sober house, it was well after dark. She approached the front door and reluctantly knocked.

"It smells like farts," she said, recalling that stuffed cabbage was on the menu for the night.

The door opened a crack and two eyes with dark bags under them stared through the crack.

"Misty?" Chelsea's raspy voice was low and comforting. "You made it! Come in, hun, we still have some leftovers and we've gotten nowhere on this puzzle."

Misty came in and sat down on the couch, in front of the puzzle. Joan gave her a microwavable plastic plate with stuffed cabbage and mashed potatoes on it, and a little iceberg salad on the side.

"My car..." Misty groaned. "Someone slashed my tires outside of Chevrolait."

"How about some iced tea, doll?" Joan asked, patting Misty on the back.

Misty ate slowly, savoring every bite of the hot meal as Chelsea argued with Joan about whether she was forcing the puzzle pieces to go together or not.

"It fits, see?" Chelsea declared.

"Like hell it does!" exclaimed Joan.

The home was warm from the heat of a peach cobbler baking in the oven. Misty was only halfway through her food before her head grew heavy and fell against the back couch as she drifted into a deep sleep.

The next morning, Misty woke up to light beaming on her face as she lay on the couch with an afghan pulled over her. She was shocked at first, forgetting where she was, but the smell of bacon and coffee comforted her as she got her bearings. She put her head back down on the pillow and took a deep breath.

"Morning, Misty," Joan said from the kitchen. "Hope we didn't wake you, I told Chelsea to go back to the bedroom with her breakfast since she can't seem to do anything without making a racket."

"No, no. I'm awake, it's okay," Misty shifted and sat upright. She yawned and rubbed the sleep from her eyes. She didn't even want to think about everything that had been going on, so she chose to just stare at the unfinished puzzle on the coffee table for a while.

"No way!"

Misty heard a shout from down the hall.

"See, there she goes again!" Joan bickered.

A door opened down the hall and out came Chelsea, holding the Cleveland Plain Dealer in her hands.

"Hey Misty! Don't you work at a coffee shop?"

"Yeah... Coffee Bucket," Misty said groggily.

Chelsea came into the living room, her eyes all bugged out and excited.

"Well you better be careful. Check this out!"

She dropped the paper on top of the puzzle and a few pieces fell to the ground.

"CLEVELAND COFFEE SHOP KILLER: SECOND BARISTA DIES FROM GUNSHOT WOUND. KILLER AT LARGE."

Below the headline was a photo of Jace.

CHAPTER TWELVE

-

COFFEE BUCKET WAS ALREADY ABUZZ with activity when Misty clocked in for her shift.

Summer was behind the counter and seemed stressed out. She wasn't really dressed in any sort of specific way and just looked disheveled, mostly. She handed Misty a milk pitcher to steam while she ground out some espresso beans to pull a shot.

"Who are these freaks! The Cleveland Coffee Killer strikes a second time and everyone decides now, all of a sudden, they need coffee. Disaster tourism at its finest." She handed Misty a hot coffee. "Here, have this, you're gonna need it. I put some vanilla and cream in it, maybe you'll like that better."

Misty didn't care much for coffee, but she took a sip anyway. It wasn't terrible, but she wasn't a fan. The cafe was full and crowded. Everyone was waiting for their coffee or sipping their lattes, many of them holding newspapers.

"Who's this cappuccino for?" Misty asked, looking at the completed drinks that Summer had made sitting on the counter.

"Jeff or Jerry...," Summer pointed to the end of the counter, "I can't remember which one is which."

Misty looked down toward the end of the counter. The retirement guys were sitting there, in their crisp button-down shirts and ties, looking like they were just as likely to convert her to the Church of Latter Day Saints than to sign her up for the company retirement plan. They waved at her simultaneously.

Misty's heart sank. The retirement plan. She still hadn't signed up for it and by the looks of the line in front of the cash register, it was unlikely she'd have time to sign up today, either.

"Cappuccino?" Misty asked as she neared the gentlemen.

"Here," Jerry, the older and shorter man said, raising his hand. "How are you today, Misty?"

"I'm good. It's freaking busy in here, though."

"Hah!" Jerry laughed. "It sure is--hey... when you have a second I'd love to go over the retirement plan with you..."

"It's free money," Jeff, the younger, taller one chimed in, grinning. "Summer's already signed up and we should be getting Mr. Larry signed on this evening. Can't wait to have you on board, Misty."

"Right, right. I promise, I will sign up as soon as I have a second."

"Americano!" Summer yelled from the espresso machine.

"Oh, that's mine," said Jeff, grinning at Misty, who ran and got his drink before returning to the cash register.

As she took customers' orders, she couldn't help but feel a little guilt at having completely forgotten about signing up for the plan. Here she was supposed to be growing up, getting her life in order, but all she kept finding herself doing was falling into the same old trouble, stalking people and getting her tires slashed.

"Mother Effer!" Misty shouted as she slammed her finger in the cash register. Just then, Detective Mills walked through the front door.

"Why, hello there, Misty. Summer," He said, skipping to the front of the line. "I'll have a Vanilla Latte when you have a second," he tapped his hand on the table a couple times and walked away without leaving any money or a card.

Misty returned to the customer who was handing her a twenty dollar bill. She had gone too many steps on the iPad and had to figure out the customer's change in her head. "Damn it..." she said under her breath.

Jeff, who was sitting close to the register said, "$14.75."

"Huh?" Misty said, looking over at him.

"Her change is $14.75. I'm kinda good with numbers," he added, with a wink.

"Thanks," Misty said, smiling awkwardly. He was handsome and tall. Misty wondered if maybe she could get him to agree to a little signing bonus for the retirement plan. The promise of a little smooch smooch might help get her through the paperwork a little easier. She took a sip of her vanilla coffee, trying to look cute and sexy in the process, but the bitter flavor, barely hidden by the sweetness of the vanilla flavor, caused her to cringe and scrunch her face.

Misty put the twenty in the drawer and handed the customer the correct change. She couldn't help but feel the heavy presence of Detective Mills hovering at the counter behind her. It reminded her of the day she started working, the day after the first Coffee Shop Killing. Misty had been in the area the night before looking for work. Luckily, Detective Mills hadn't figured that out yet, or so it seemed. But it didn't make her feel good seeing him in the coffee shop today, considering she had been stalking the second victim of the Cleveland Coffee Shop Killer on the night of his death, too. Shit. This looked real bad.

Misty brought the Vanilla Latte to Detective Mills, who stood at the counter next to Jerry and Jeff, the retirement guys and a couple other patrons who seemed more thirsty for drama than coffee.

"All I can tell you is that the victim was shot. A different murder than the first one, but since the two victims were both coffee shop baristas and had been acquainted with each other, we believe the murders are related."

"No, duh," thought Misty. "This guy is a real genius. Just dumb enough to believe I did it, if he ever gets that far."

"Some people heard a woman screaming profanities outside the victim's workplace the evening of the murder. Said she was screaming in a broken down silver Corolla. We're looking into it."

"Shit."

"Another person insisted it was a burly man. With a mustache. Whoever it was, we'll find them."

Misty rolled her eyes. The Corolla. She had to leave her car there last night after someone slashed the tires and messed with the engine. Who had done that? Misty wondered. And why?

She thought about her stupid, banged up, junky Corolla, sitting there outside of Chevrolait. Chances are the police were ID'ing the vehicle at that very moment. She was screwed. She took a deep breath. They can prove I was there, but they can't prove I murdered Jace. I'll be okay. But I probably will get arrested. Oh, God.

Misty felt like she was going to vomit. She just wanted to run away and escape. What had she gotten herself into?

A few hours into the shift, the door jingled open.

"Hi, what can I get for you today?" Misty said, unenthusiastically without looking up.

"I'll take a nice hot cup of tea with a side of more tea," a familiar voice said.

Misty looked up and Tramaine stood with her D&D notebook in her hand, waving it back and forth.

"I actually want coffee, not tea. But I do have some serious tea to spill with you, Misty. Oh, boy," Tramaine said. "I wanted to tell you last night, but you were totally passed out by the time I got home. These anarchists are shady, Misty. And all is not well in aquaponics land, let me tell you. They were scared of the cops investigating them and people finding out about something they did. Grover seemed the most worried. I wonder if we can get some information out of him."

A group of three customers came into the shop, loudly laughing. Misty made note of Tramaine's information and excused herself. Tramaine's enthusiasm was promising, but Misty really couldn't even imagine continuing her investigation. She felt so lost and overwhelmed and now she was going to have to make three drinks for these customers. She just wanted to escape. She took a sip of coffee, winced and greeted the customers.

As her shift came to a close, Misty sat at a table with Jeff and Jerry, who'd agreed to meet her near the end of her shift. At the very least she'd get to start the process of setting up her employment benefits.

Jerry was detailing the numbers and how the plan works, how much would be set aside and how much the employer would match. Misty looked at the paper and the numbers all started spinning. She couldn't stop thinking, worrying about being arrested and ending up back in jail. She kept looking behind her back, over her shoulder and all around the coffee shop--paranoid that at any moment Detective Mills would be cuffing her and reading her rights.

"Does that all make sense, Misty?"

Misty didn't hear Jerry. Her mind was elsewhere and she was just trying to see straight.

"Misty?"

"I think I need a glass of water..." Misty rushed to the bathroom. As soon as she reached the toilet she immediately blew chunks of last night's stuffed cabbage all over the place.

Out in the cafe, Jerry and Jeff looked at each other. They could hear her retching loudly in the bathroom, as could the rest of the patrons of the cafe.

Summer knocked on the door. "Misty, honey?" She let herself in. "Misty, you can finish the paperwork another day. Why don't you just go home and get some rest. Mr. Larry is here and can take over."

"Misty? It's Mr. Larry," came a kind and rattling older man's voice. "I have some cough drops in my sweater. Would you like one?"

The walk back to the sober house did little to calm Misty's nerves. She was in a complete daze as she made her way down the street. Someone had killed Jace, her primary suspect, not long after she had confronted him. Did the killer know Misty was talking with Jace? Jace claimed he wasn't involved in whatever Vanessa was involved in. Was he telling the truth? Why had the Cleveland Coffee Killer targeted Vanessa and Jace? Misty needed answers.

But would she even have time to investigate before she herself got arrested? All she could think about was how the cops were running her plates and on their way to pick her up. It's probably a good thing she wasn't at the coffee shop signing up for retirement, because that's where the police knew to find her. She just had to hope that whoever was working at the cafe didn't rat out her location at the sober house.

Back at home, Misty showered off and brushed the vomit out of her teeth. She still didn't feel all that well, but agreed to join in a game of Settlers of Catan with her housemates.

"Okay, Misty," Tramaine tried to explain the rules to the new player. "On your turn you roll the die and then we'll see who gets resources."

Misty rolled the die.

"Great, you rolled a seven. So that means I get three lumber, Joan gets three lumber and Chelsea gets two bricks."

"What do I get?"

"Well, since you don't have any property adjacent to the number seven, you don't get any resources."

Misty hadn't understood the game at all up to this point. It seemed to her that the game was just everybody else getting to do stuff and she just gets to do jack shit. And she was probably gonna get arrested soon. Misty flipped the game board and the pieces went flying everywhere.

"Fuck that!" she yelled before storming out the front door with tears in her eyes.

"This is bullshit," she thought to herself. "Stupid fucking game. I hate those bitches."

Her eyes were wet with tears, but as she made her way toward the front house she noticed something familiar in the driveway.

"What the fuck? Is that my Corolla? What the fuck is going on?" she yelled out loud.

Tramaine came out of the back house.

"Misty, are you all right, hun?"

"What's my car doing here?" Misty's paranoia was at an all-time high. Were her own roommates in on this with the cops? Why was her car here when she had left it at Chevrolait the night before?

"You told us it was stuck at the coffee shop last night. Gus went and towed it back here."

"Gus?" Misty was pissed. "I didn't ask you to do that?"

"I know. We just didn't want you to have your car stuck."

"I don't need your help and I definitely don't need Gus's help!"

Misty was irate and in tears. She knew it was good that her car wasn't there anymore, but she was pissed that stupid Gus had helped her. "Fuck this shit."

Just then, Gus made his way out of the back door of his house and out onto the porch.

"That car is fried, Misty," he said.

"What do you know, jackass?" she shouted.

"I know that you're better off selling it for parts. I can sell it for you if you want. I have a bike you can use in the meantime," he added, pointing to a BMX bike leaning against the porch.

"You probably fucked it up when you towed it over here," she said.

"Come on, Misty, we're only trying to help you out," Tramaine said.

"No one asked, Tramaine! Give me that stupid bike," Misty shouted. "I'm out of here!"

Misty needed answers and she didn't have time to spare. Vanessa was involved in something shady with the anarchists. Misty was going to find out exactly what that was and nothing was going to stop her.

She awkwardly pedaled the BMX bike past her banged up Corolla and out onto the street, her ass crack fully exposed to the blustery fall air.

CHAPTER THIRTEEN

—

Cleveland Aquaponics' headquarters were far enough away that Misty was exhausted and sweating by the time she got there.

When she walked in, the three employees of the company were spread out. Big Ben was in the open garage door shoveling compost. Michelle was in the central glass room on her laptop and Grover was sprawled out over a drafting table working on design plans for another living wall. Misty approached the table.

"Excuse me, hello," she said, meekly, casually wiping the sweat from her forehead. "I'm here for a tour?"

It was an idea that worked when Misty visited Jace at the coffee roastery, so she figured why not give it a try here.

Grover looked up, a little confused. "Hi. A tour?"

"Yeah, I emailed a while ago. I'm visiting from Columbus..." Misty just threw it out there, hoping that maybe she sounded official if she referenced the state capitol.

"Oh," Grover huffed. "I'm the last to know anything around here. It would be nice to be updated about things every once in a while, but I guess I can just fend for myself. Anyway, I'll show you around."

Grover walked Misty to the living wall.

"This wall is a representation of the utility of the aquaponics system I designed. Here, we have an assortment of plants and vegetables that can be grown in a vertical fashion without the necessity of soil. This economizes space and uses less water, as the root systems are regularly sprayed with a fine mist, instead of doused in water, most of which would drain away."

Misty admired the wall.

"What makes our aquaponics system different from others is our unique, patented design. As you can see, the back of the wall is made up of a fine mesh. The mesh is actually reminiscent of an underground mycorrhizal network. I engineered this material so that moisture will easily flow through the mesh to any dry areas, ensuring that all plants on the wall receive the level of moisture they need. You know it's a Cleveland Aquaponics wall if you see the shiny blue-tinted mesh."

Grover pulled a piece of lettuce off the wall and handed it to Misty.

"Go ahead, taste it," he said.

Misty stared at the bright green leaf in her hand. "Doesn't this usually go on a burger or something?"

"Hah!" Grover said, the curls of his moustache turning up right in a smile. "Yeah, I'll see what we can do."

After a pause, he added somewhat timidly, "You know, you're not the only one who hates vegetables..." He took Misty to another display which showed the exposed inner workings of the watering system.

"We don't sell a lot of walls for growing food," he clarified. He looked disappointed. "A majority of our sales are to big corporations who want huge aquaponic walls in the lobby's of their buildings, purely for aesthetics and optics. We sell them the design, installation and maintenance. And sadly, we've agreed to also water their potted plants while we're there. We're trying to diversify the business so we can better make a difference, but right now... I don't even know."

They approached Big Ben, who sat in a small front loader wearing overalls without a shirt.

"This is Big Ben. He's helping us develop our compost business, to help cut down on food waste."

Misty looked down at the lettuce in her hand.

"Throw it in the pile," Big Ben said, pointing to the compost pile on the concrete floor. "Oh yeah, she's gonna like that."

"Basically, we're trying our best to figure out how we can be a green company and use our position to actually help people in the world..." Grover said the last part with a little added volume.

A door slammed and everyone looked over to the small room as Michelle rounded a corner.

"I can hear you, jackass!" Michelle announced, completely disregarding their new guest.

"This is Michelle," Grover said. "She helps us with the money stuff. We're making plenty of it, but there are only so many walls in office buildings and not all of them can be decorative living walls, so I'm not sure where we go from here."

"You know, I don't appreciate that. I work very hard," she looked at Misty. They were almost in identical outfits. But while Misty was wearing an XXL Outer Banks souvenir t-shirt and Starter brand basketball shorts, Michelle's T-shirt was Balenciaga and her shorts were Dior. She looked Misty up and down, pausing at Misty's flip-flops that she stole from the Gap.

"Nice outfit. Dolce & Gabbana?" Michelle asked.

Misty shook her head. "Dave & Busters," she replied.

Michelle nodded respectfully as Grover continued: "I'm not saying you don't work hard, Michelle. But who are you working for, is the real question."

"You know, I may be in finance, but I am helping people. Real people. My full time job is in private equity which I use to help finance small businesses through grants and such. It's a redistribution of power and resources. Maybe I'm not shoving my dick in compost all day, but I am actually helping the world."

"Hey! We do not shove our dicks in compost all day," Grover was offended and looked to Big Ben for reassurance. "Right, Ben?"

"Not all day," Big Ben responded.

"It wouldn't hurt you to lend a hand and turn the compost every once in a while. You may get some dirt on your Chanel socks or whatever, but I'm sure the dry cleaners could get that out if you paid them enough."

"How many times do I have to explain this. Anarchism and a just world doesn't mean everyone has to be poor and tasteless. It just means the structures aren't manipulated to deliberately redistribute wealth. Don't be ignorant."

"In anarcho-communism there is no property and there is no money," Ben added. "So anyone who wanted Chanel socks could just go get Chanel socks."

Michelle rolled her eyes. "You know, I'd like a little more respect around here. You literally would not be a functioning company without my help. My continued help. Without me, you'd still be rigging up PVC pipe in your basement studio apartment to water your basil."

"Let's go," Grover said, lightly putting his hand on Misty's lower back and walking her to a door in the back of the warehouse. Through the door was a stairwell. Misty sluggishly followed him up five flights of stairs to the top floor of the warehouse. He opened another door, revealing a large loft apartment, full of natural light and plants and fountains.

"Wow," Misty said, taking it all in. "Is this where you live?"

"Yep. So much for work-life balance," Grover said, as he sat at another drafting table littered with graph paper and sketches. "So, is this an interview or something? We do a lot of interviews. Is there any chance I can convince you not to write about that blow-up down there?"

"Oh, no," Misty said. "I'm not a reporter. I can barely spell and I'm definitely, like, not grammar at all."

Grover laughed. "Well, a lot of people think that this work is just some sort of utopia. Like we're saving the planet and it's all just mushrooms and rainbows and massage circles. In a way I don't even care if people see the conflict. It's like compost. Sometimes good stuff smells like shit. I just wish there were a little less bullshit, but it is what it is."

Misty walked through the apartment, admiring the vintage furniture and eclectic decorations. Grover leaned against a wooden ladder casually, yet somewhat rehearsed. He may not be wearing designer clothing, but his look was just as deliberate as Michelle's. He looked like he lived on a permaculture commune where he practiced glass blowing and whittled wooden pipes to play in the commune jug band.

But he didn't. He owned a business and he lived in a 1200 square foot loft with 10 foot ceilings.

He was the kind of guy who resented that he wasn't missing a front tooth, but was too cautious of a person to put himself in a situation that might result in losing one.

"I just want the world to be a better place," he said, depressingly.

"Maybe you could get a job at Disney World." Misty asked. She was admiring some of the art on the walls, concert posters and photographs of mushrooms.

"Hah! Right. The world would be a much better place without huge corporations like Disney. They're just distracting everyone from real issues and paying slave wages and creating false expectations that result in kids being depressed."

"The Parent Trap did fuck me up. I'm starting to think maybe I don't even have a rich British twin."

"Hah! I hear you, though. Everybody is just obsessed with being rich. And if you want to do something that actually contributes to society, if you don't have money to do it, you need investors to get started. People think what I'm doing is good, but I don't even know anymore. Maybe I should just run off into the woods and leave this all behind."

"If you want to leave for a while, I can watch your apartment for you for pretty cheap," Misty said, eyeing up the place. "Where's the TV?"

"I don't have a TV. I'm not trying to get brainwashed. I like being able to think for myself, thank you."

"You ever lighten up? Maybe you're hangry. You look hangry. When's the last time you ate?" Misty was in the kitchen. She opened the refrigerator door and saw a half full case of Miller High Life, a jar of mayonnaise and an empty pizza box. "What the hell? Where's your food? You got a secret food wall up here, too?" She knocked on the walls listening for a hollow spot.

Grover grabbed two of the cans of beer. He opened one and gave it to Misty.

"I know, I know. I'm a little too serious... and a bit of a workaholic.

I just... I just want to do my part. I want to do whatever I can to help dismantle capitalism and help our society get its priorities right. I'm just stressed because I'm worried I'm not doing it right."

"Well, who the fuck are you anyway? The president of America? Jesus. Give it a rest, dude. You got a bottle opener?" Misty opened and closed the drawers in his kitchen, shuffling through them."

"It's a can."

"I know," she finally found a can opener and pulled it out. "You're shotgunning this one," she added, taking the unopened can from the refrigerator and puncturing a hole in the bottom. "Hit it, bro."

Grover grinned, shook his head and then cracked open the top and sucked the High Life out of the can. "Whew!" he shouted. "Been a while!"

"Fuck yah!" Misty smashed her can between her hands.

"There's a recycling bin under the sink," Grover said.

"Fuck that!" Misty opened a window and threw the can outside.

"Come on! Why did you do that? That's littering!"

"Fuck that shit! Who are you? President Harrison Ford on Air Force One? Give me a break, dude!"

"No, no. You're right, you're right. I'm... I'm doing the best I can... sometimes in order to help the planet you have to work with the people that hurt it. I wish we could do it without money or power, but that's just not how things work."

"If you say so, bro," Misty grabbed a few more cans. It had been a while since she'd had a drink. She hadn't had time to drink since she'd gotten out of jail. She'd been too busy trying to deal with all the bullshit going on since she got out. Then she agreed to live in the sober house and drinking while living there was a serious no-no. She stared at the can.

"If I get some Altoids on the way home no one will even know..." she thought. They were the ones that asked her to lie in order to live there anyway. "It's just one beer and they probably won't even care, anyway."

But after she slammed that first can, she was thirsty for more.

Grover repositioned to the couch. The afternoon light was diffused by the hanging plants in the window, basking him in an earthy glow. He waited for Misty to join him there. After she sat down, Grover looked off toward, but not directly at the exposed kitchen.

"You know, I get a lot of attention for my work. I thought you were a reporter because a lot of people want to interview me about my successful green business. But I have a reason for doing what I do and it isn't for the fame or the attention or the respect. I haven't shared this with a lot of people, but... my reason... it's really quite poetic, actually."

He turned on the couch to face Misty. He stared into her eyes. His voice changed as he delivered to her his poetic manifesto. He sounded like he was giving a presentation in a high school English class.

"I see myself as a steward of the land. Its caretaker.

Her bounty not mine for the taking, but mine for the cultivating.

'Tis not noble.

'Tis not a sacrifice.

My country knows no borders but those between land and sea, mountain peak and low valley, dry desert and lush oasis.

That, THEREFORE, is why I do this.

Because to me, what else is there for to do?

But for to CARE for the sake of LIFE,

In all its glory.

ALL. ITS. glory.

Glory unto the land.

For THAT is from whence I came.

And THAT is from whence where will I return."

Grover continued to stare at Misty, though his eyes were now closed. He slowly lowered his head before opening his eyes and taking a deep breath. He shook out his hands and sighed a sigh of relief.

"I wrote that myself, actually."

"Oh. You wrote that. Well... that is..." Misty searched around in her head for the right word. "Gay. Not really my thing. You lost me when you kept saying "'tis." It made me think of tits, actually. Then you said mountains and valleys and lush oasis. I was just picturing bouncing boobies in my head and to be honest I think I started to develop a little lush oasis in my panties if you know what I mean. After that, I didn't hear another word you said until you said "I came" and I was like... whoa, there, big fella, I'm just getting started..."

Grover stared at Misty. It wasn't the first time anyone had had such a visceral reaction to his poetry. Or a combination of his poetry, his pungent pheremones and/or riveting bachelor pad.

"Sorry. I just haven't had sex in a long time," Misty admitted.

"Really?"

"Nope. Everyone in jail was a prude and since I got out I've just been kind of distracted and stuff..."

He stared at her. Misty could see each individual rib piercing out from underneath his sweat stained wife beater, threatening to puncture it with every heaving breath. His full black beard was adorned with pieces of partially chewed cabbage and carrot. His lips were... somewhere in there. She mostly got a lot of hair when she kissed him.

He fell back on to the couch, pulling her with him. His tongue caressed her lips as he kissed her repeatedly, fully making out. He rolled her to the side and she fell with her back to the floor, knocking over a nearby potted draecana. Grover was now on top of her. He arched his back to take in full view of Misty. She lay there, her face flush. Underneath her oversized tie-dye Outer Banks souvenir t-shirt her oversized and unrestrained breasts cascaded to either side. She wiggled out of the shirt, revealing herself and the thorny rose and majestic horse tattoos on her side.

"I like your tattoos," said Grover. "I hear the ribs are one of the most painful places to get one."

"Maybe for you," Misty said as she pulled Grover's wife beater over his head. A cloud of dust exploded in the sunlight as the shirt tossled Grover's unwashed hair.

He ran his tongue over her nipple and it grew hard as goosebumps sprung up around it and up to her neck, releasing an ecstatic sigh from Misty's mouth. He sat up and brought his hands to his navel, which was covered by a jungle of thick hair, leading down into his tight black denim jeans. He began to unbutton his pants. Misty stopped him, grabbing his head and positioning it back on her breasts. "Not so fast, kemosabe," she said.

Her bounty was his, not for the taking. But for the cultivating. He was going to have to spend some time caring for the glory of her "'tis" before anything else.

Grover was good at that part and had no trouble giving Misty's breasts some special attention. However, Grover's enthusiasm wasn't without some limits.

"You're telling me you can't slap my ass?" Misty said, as they rolled around on Grover's soft, fancy rug.

"I... I just couldn't do that," Grover said, definitely.

"But my ass..." Misty objected. "Look at it... there's so much to slap..."

Misty was offended. There really was a lot to slap and once it was, it would put on a real show, shaking and jiggling seemingly without end. Misty's ass was like one of Gus's old cars: a Chevy pickup. All you had to do to get it going was give it a good smack on the hood.

"What are you willing to do to my nipples? Will you bite them?" Misty asked.

"No. I can lick them," Grover replied. "Tenderly."

Misty rolled her eyes. "Can I slap you?"

"No!" Grover said, shocked.

"Just for fun! Christ!" Misty shrugged it off.

"Okay, let's just kiss again for a little bit and maybe suck my tongue a little less," Grover continued. "And maybe let's move to my bed. The floor is kinda uncomfortable and I have a nice mattress from Dick Vagantis Cleveland Mattress."

"Yeesh," Misty gasped. "You know, I've got an idea of something that would really turn you on."

"Oh, really?" Grover inquired, eagerly. "What?"

"Why don't you and me just sit here and we can play patty cake until one of us has an orgasm. How's that sound?"

Grover rolled his eyes.

"All right, I get it. You can suck on my tongue."

Misty lay on the shag rug on the floor, her head beside the shag rug on Grover's face. He held his phone above his face and placed an order for a pizza delivery. After a while Misty broke the silence.

"Did you know Vanessa Bergeron?" Misty asked. Grover let out a sigh.

"Oh, so that's why you're here," Grover lay on his back. He raised his hands and wove them through his long, dirty hair.

"I'm just a friend of hers. I'm not a cop or anything. I'm just looking for some answers, to see if anyone knows anything."

"You were friends with her, huh? If you think I'm serious, you must have had a real fun time with Vanessa. She was more serious than I am."

Misty lay there, thinking about how little she really knew of Vanessa. She interacted with her briefly on the night of the murder. Vanessa seems irritated and frustrated. She certainly wasn't warm and welcoming.

"Vanessa was more critical of me than I am of myself and that's saying a lot." Grover must have been reflecting on his time with Vanessa, too. "I'm sure you know she came to our anarchist book club. In a lot of ways she and I agreed. We were both sick of capitalism and wanted to do whatever we could to dismantle it and build something better. Something less violent."

Grover turned over on his side.

"Vanessa and I shared a passion and urgency that I don't see much of. Big Ben seems to care more about the planet than about people or governments. He's so patient it seems like he's just waiting for society to collapse and leave the planet alone. Michelle is strategic. It seems like she's more about the chess game than anything else. But I don't feel like this is a game. I see people hurting or suffering and I feel like we need to do something now. And I know that's how Vanessa felt, too. She and I shared an urgent sense of responsibility. What could we do ourselves to make change?"

"What was Vanessa doing? Was she involved in Aquatonis?"

"Aquaponics? Hah! Definitely not," Grover sat up and put his back against the couch. He tied his hair up in a man-bun. "Vanessa hated my business. I don't blame her. She was critical of working within the system. She believed in direct action. She wanted to undermine capitalism directly, in whatever way she could. She resented it. The last thing she would do is start a business with funding from financers. She thought we were sell-outs and hypocrites. And she was disgusted at the way other members of the book club looked up to us."

"Why?"

"She hated traditional power dynamics. She didn't think we deserved authority or attention just because we started a business and got attention from mainstream media outlets."

"If Vanessa hated you all so much why did she hang out with you?"

"Well... because we're trying. It's what I liked about Vanessa. She didn't expect a fair society to be easy or for everyone to just all get along. She just wanted it to be more fair and less oppressive. She worked with us because we were trying. And, oh yeah, maybe for another pretty important reason..."

Just then Grover's phone buzzed with a notification.

"What reason?" Misty asked, with anticipation.

"Pizza's here!" Grover smiled. "I'll be right back."

Grover got up, slipped on some old sneakers and pranced back into the stairwell and down the stairs.

Misty had gotten some juicy information. And some ass on top of that. And Grover was about to come back up the stairs not just with a hot slice of pizza but another hot slice of information that could help lead Misty to Vanessa's real killer.

CHAPTER FOURTEEN

-

"She was selling drugs."

Misty lifted Tramaine's cup and scrubbed the countertop underneath it. She was feeling invigorated. She just had sex and she finally had some solid, juicy information about Vanessa that no one else knew about.

"I'm a detective," Misty said proudly. "And a whore. I'm a whore detective. Sucking dick and taking names."

"Well, that is something." Tramaine said, nodding her head. "I'm glad you looked into it. I knew there was something going on with the anarchists. So do you think they're involved in drugs?"

Tramaine's memory was flashing back to eavesdropping on the argument at the aquaponics headquarters, her heart racing. Tramaine rarely ventured far from the sober house. She preferred to get her excitement in fantasy form. She desperately wanted to be like her role-playing character, Snake, in real life, but rarely had she come close to having Snake's audacity. Climbing that plant wall had proven to Tramaine that maybe she was more like Snake than she even realized.

"Grover didn't mention anything about himself being involved with drugs, so I don't know about that. But him and the other people are definitely pissed at each other. There's some shady shit going on with them, especially with that aquasizing company. I mean what kind of business is that, anyway? I'm no Billy Mays, but vegetables on a wall and piles of dirt? It sure as hell ain't OxiClean. There's got to be more going on there."

"Whatever it is, they're stressed out about it--I can guarantee that."

"So Vanessa was selling drugs and Grover admitted that he was the one that introduced Vanessa to the drug dealers... I think maybe he felt guilty about it. I wonder if he thinks the reason Vanessa was murdered might be related to the drug cartel."

Misty couldn't remember and likely couldn't even comprehend the specific details from the night before, but over post-coital pizza and beer, Grover had admitted that, "Vanessa wanted to take more direct action against capitalism. She said she was thinking about getting involved in the black market or some other non-taxed form of commerce, since taxes only went to fund the military industrial complex. She felt that even if the resources were drugs, it was still better to keep them flowing within the community rather than giving all our money to Washington DC or multi-national corporations."

Grover had connections to a drug operation and he got high off the feeling of helping others; it made him feel like he was needed and had power. So when Vanessa came to him desperate and looking for help, he couldn't resist introducing Vanessa to that world. He gave her the number of one of the drug dealers he knew and notified his contact that she was looking for some work.

"But that was it. I gave her the number and left it at that. She told me she started working for them, but I'm worried that maybe she got in over her head... I know I did," he added, cryptically.

The cafe was mostly empty, but they were still talking to each other in low voices.

"Did the drug cartel have a name?" Tramaine asked.

Misty shook her head. "Not that I know of. But I'm going to find out more. Trust that. Come with me tonight."

"Where?"

"I got the number of the drug dealer that brought Vanessa into the business. I placed an order."

"What? What did you order?"

"Just weed. Ordered a quarter. I'm meeting her tonight at the Aldi parking lot on Lorain for the handoff. I want to tail her, but I just have a bike."

"You're going to follow the drug dealer? Where, back to her apartment?"

"Sure. And then I can keep tabs on her and find out where she goes to get the drugs. Or maybe she'll go right back to the drug warehouse or whatever tonight. I don't know, but I set up this meeting and I don't want to waste it. I need to get all the information I can get. Maybe I'll try to sleep with her. My plan is that I'll bike there and then you'll already be there in a car and after the handoff, I'll join you in the car and we'll follow her."

"What car? I don't have a car, Misty. I don't drive!"

Misty stared at Tramaine. Tramaine stared back. "What?" she asked.

"Never mind," Misty replied.

Summer inched over to Misty and Tramaine.

"You know, I'm not trying to hear what you guys are talking about, but when I heard you say 'drugs' it made it kind of hard not to listen in."

Misty and Tramaine just looked at one another.

"Whatever you're getting up to, Misty, please be safe. The Cleveland Coffee Killer is out there and I don't want you ending up in any danger." Summer inched closer and whispered. "Do you need a gun?"

Misty and Tramaine just looked at each other before bursting out into laughter.

After work, Misty took her bike home and walked it down the driveway past Gus's line-up of cars in various states and conditions. She locked her bike up to the fence. Misty looked up at the sky. Dark clouds were rolling in and a strong wind was blowing through the trees. It was loud outside. A storm was coming.

Misty sighed and walked up the porch stairs to Gus's back door and knocked.

"Come in!" Gus yelled from inside.

Misty walked through the back door into the kitchen. The room was no more organized than the backyard. Pizza boxes sat open on the counter, empty beer cans on every surface and cardboard boxes of junk sat on the floor.

"Shit..." Misty said, looking around the kitchen, trying to figure out if there was any clear organization to the place. She slyly opened a couple of the kitchen drawers. "Where you at?" she called out.

"I'm in the bathroom!" Gus replied.

"Well, fuck... it can wait, I guess," Misty called back, still milling around the back door.

"I'm not on the toilet, I'm installing a bidet!"

"A what?" Misty asked.

Gus turned the corner and stood in the doorway with a tube in one hand and a wrench in the other. He was shirtless and wearing cargo shorts and ankle-high sand colored construction boots with white knee socks.

"I'm puttin' in a bidet. Sprays your ass with water so you don't have to scrape the shit off with paper. Better for your anal health and you don't get dingleberries. You could probably use one, Misty. I know you've always been hard on your anus. I'll install one in the other house once I get done with this one."

"You don't know shit about my anus. I haven't had blood in my stool in months, so you can keep your bidet and shove it up your wet and healthy ass."

"What's up? How's life in the sober house?"

"It's fine. Smells like cabbage. I think Tramaine talks in her sleep or something. But it's cool."

Misty looked around, nervously. "I need to borrow a car."

"You want to borrow one of my cars?" Gus smiled.

"Yes. I need it, just for tonight."

"What do you think I'm going to say?" Gus leaned against the doorframe.

"No."

"Bingo."

"Come on! Why?"

"Because you suck at driving and you don't know how to care for a vehicle. You run cars into the ground, girl. You aim for potholes. I don't want your hands or feet touching any one of my pretty babies. You know that. When you're in my car, I don't even want you turning the dial on the radio. Some things about me may change, babe, but 'my cars, my rules' doesn't change. That solid as rock. Strong as it can be. Like a Chevy Silverado."

"Fuck you! I'm a good driver! It's just for tonight, please? You stole my car!"

"Misty, I helped you out. Your car was fucked up. Someone slit the tires, they cut the breaks and the transmission was completely destroyed. Not to mention the catalytic converter. You could hear your car, right? Because everyone within a half-mile radius could hear your car."

Misty's heart was pounding. For one thing, she still didn't know who had destroyed her car and why. On top of that, who did Gus think he was, just deciding that her car was out of commission without even asking her what she wanted to do. She looked around his stupid house. It wasn't even cute. It looked like a college dorm. A ratty old couch. A big screen TV. An Xbox.

"Where'd you get that Xbox?" Misty asked, with a tinge of jealous fury in her voice. Gus didn't answer the question.

"You know Toyotas are supposed to run forever, so I don't know what you did to ruin yours, but good job. That takes skill."

"Shut up," Misty said.

"Anyways, I told you I'd sell it for you. There's $600 cash on your bed in your bedroom if you haven't found it yet. I ripped them off to get that much to be honest. Felt guilty and went to church afterwards."

Misty was pissed. She didn't like having conflicting feelings. But her car wasn't running and now she had $600 in cash. She wanted to run to her bedroom right at that moment and smell the cash. She was excited, but she tried to suppress a smile, because she was still mad at Gus.

"I didn't ask for your help," she said, stubbornly.

"No, just my car."

A crack of lightning flashed through the window.

Misty's face turned red with rage. "Fuck you!" she screamed. She stormed past him into the front room. She picked a lamp up off the floor, turned around and threw it at Gus. He dodged it and turned around as it flew past him and into the wall. He leaned down and picked it up, turning back to Misty. "Doesn't work anyway," he said, holding up the lamp.

But Misty was already on the front porch, the screen door slamming behind her. Thunder crashed in the sky as Misty ran out into the rain and turned back down the driveway. If she had just gone out the back door, she wouldn't have gotten as soaked by the rain. But if she went out the back door, she wouldn't have been able to walk past the line of keys hanging on the wall in the living room.

When she got to her bedroom, she opened her hand and looked down at the keys to the 1987 Toyota Celica that was parked on the street in the front of the house. She grabbed the envelope off her pillow and smiled. "Jackpot," she said as she thumbed through the bills inside.

Misty changed into dry clothes and stole a raincoat and umbrella from the closet in the hallway, then snuck out the front door and up the driveway. She quietly got into the car and waited patiently. Lightning flashed in the sky. Her hand was on the key in the ignition. A few seconds later as the sky boomed with a loud roll of thunder, Misty turned the key and fired up the Celica. She rolled down the street, without anyone knowing a thing.

The tall lights in the Aldi plaza parking lot illuminated the rain as it poured down. It's not the location Misty would have chosen for a drug handoff, given that the last time she was here she was arrested for assaulting her old boss from Pizza Fever. It left her feeling anxious and a little paranoid as she scanned the parking lot for squad cars and the car of this dealer.

The dealer said she'd be driving a black Honda Civic Type R, whatever that meant. Almost every car was black. Misty worried that Gus's gold Celica would stand out, but hopefully with the storm there wouldn't be anyone looking around for a drug handoff.

Nevertheless, given her record, it was better for Misty to be safe than sorry. This was Cleveland, Ohio, not Venice Beach, California. Marijuana was illegal here and could land you in prison or at the very least, result in you going to jail and having your coochie violated as they look up it with a flashlight searching for more drugs.

Misty drove the perimeter of the lot. The windshield wipers on high did their best to keep the windshield clear. The plaza housed not just an Aldi, but a few other stores as well, including a Sally Beauty Supply, a Pizza Hut, a Wing Stop and a Rainbow clothing store. In the center of the lot, toward the front was a McDonalds. The busy drive-through was glowing with a row of headlights, which Misty figured would make her activity less noticeable.

Soon, Misty noticed a woman in a black raincoat standing by a trash can underneath the overhang that covered the sidewalk between the storefronts. She was standing near a black sedan that was still running. The slick car had green neon lights illuminating underneath it and the headlights were bright with a blue tint.

"Must be her," Misty thought as she pulled into an empty space on the other side of the lot. She didn't want them to see what car she was driving. She pulled the hood over her head and rushed out of the car and under the roof, then walked down the row of stores, stopping to look into a few windows in order to act casual. Eventually she reached the stranger by the trash can.

"How's it going?" she asked the stranger.

"I have that toilet paper you were looking for," the stranger said.

"Toilet paper?" Misty thought.

The stranger took out a thick roll of toilet paper and handed it to Misty. Misty looked it over. Stuffed inside the paper tube in the middle was a clear zip-lock baggie. "Ahhhh," she thought.

"Ah, yes," said Misty. "The toilet paper. I've been meaning to try this toilet paper but I can't seem to get my hands on it anywhere.

Thanks for letting me borrow a roll."

"Anytime. I hope it works out for you. Do you have the babysitting money you owe me?" asked the stranger.

"Babysitting money?" Misty thought, giving the stranger a stare. The stranger stared back and held out their hand. "What the fu-- Oh!"

"Oh, yes. Thanks for babysitting the kids for me," Misty fumbled in the pocket of her jeans for her cash. "My husband and I really needed the night off so we could go see the show on Broadway and have our fancy steak dinner downtown. I hope Shelby.... and Ian weren't too much trouble for you."

Her pants were tight and wet so she had some trouble getting the money out.

"Shelby can be such a little bitch these days, what with cheerleading tryouts coming up," Misty continued to fumble around. "Got the bank on my ass about our second mortgage and my retirement plan is overloading..." Misty's brain was shorting out on family-life speak. She finally found the cash and handed it over.

"But with my tupperware sales job on the side I think everything will turn out fine and we'll have our above-ground pool installed in no time," she smiled and heaved a sigh of relief.

"All right, then," said the stranger. "See you later."

"See ya," Misty replied. She turned and walked back towards her car. She looked behind her and noticed that the dealer was gone, but the car was still in its parking spot. Misty picked up her pace a little bit and tried to hurry to her car, so she could get there before the Honda Civic Type R pulled out. Misty needed to get as much information as she could and besides, she wanted to see first hand what Vanessa was involved in. What could she say? She was a nosey detective whore.

Misty started the Celica and the headlights rose out of the front hood.

"Sick," Misty thought to herself. Whatever you said about Gus, he did have sick taste.

The Honda Civic R Type was pulling out of the parking lot, onto a side street, heading North. Misty backed out of the space and drove quickly through the rain toward the exit.

She tailed the car through the tight one way streets of the neighborhood behind the Aldi. She knew the streets well, since her Aunt used to live and babysit in this neighborhood.

They moved slow--Misty peeking her car out slowly just to glimpse the back bumper of the Honda as it took a turn and another turn, it's blue headlights illuminating the dimly lit back streets.

Like a pit viper, Misty wove back and forth through the grid, taking shortcuts down alleyways, always cautious to not be seen. As she approached the end of an alley, she cut off her lights just in time to watch as the Honda Civic R Type rolled in front of her, unawares of her car's presence in the darkness between houses and dumpsters.

She prowled the alleyways like a cat stalking its prey: a little weed-dealing mouse that would hopefully lead her to the nest of the rat king where the cat would find out information about the cat whose job she replaced after it was murdered.

The Celica was an automatic, but Misty gripped the gear shift anyway, just in case she needed to pull a quick reverse or slam on the emergency brake for some other flashy maneuver. Maybe a "jackknife." Is that a car trick? It sounds like it could be and Misty was prepared to jackknife her ass off if she needed to.

The cars approached 117th street--a busier road that ran North to Lake Erie and south to I-71. The Honda turned North.

The street was wide, with two lanes going each direction and was much more populated than the narrow lanes of the neighborhood. The Honda increased its speed, weaving in and out of the other vehicles driving cautiously through the storm. Misty's foot got heavier, too, as she tried to keep pace, her hand gripping the gear shift even tighter.

The streetlights flickered past as Misty tried to maintain an inconspicuous distance, but stayed close enough to the car so that she wouldn't get caught at a stop light. As they approached Detroit Road, Misty anticipated the Honda would turn right, so she switched lanes to prepare, leaving a minivan in between her and the Honda. But as they reached the intersection, the Honda slowed until the light turned yellow, after which it sped straight through, leaving Misty and the minivan stuck at the red light.

"Damn it!" Misty yelled, trying to figure out what she would do. Certainly they were still headed to the highway, Misty was sure of that.

She jerked the car to the left. There were only a few cars at the intersection. She waited for an opening, then took an illegal right turn from the left lane, passing in front of the minivan, which honked angrily at her. Misty hoped she was driving parallel to the Honda which must have been one street over.

She increased her speed and dashed down Detroit toward the entrance to the Shoreway, which ran along the lake. She got to the entrance of the Shoreway and slowed down. It was difficult to see every single car through the rain and hard to tell which was which, but Misty had been tailing this Honda for long enough to have a good read on it.

She waited patiently. It had to be coming this way. Her light turned green, but there were no cars behind her so she just waited in the street. A vehicle approached from behind her. She would have to get on the Shoreway soon enough.

Just then blue light shone on the street to her left, turning onto the Shoreway. It was the Honda. As soon as it landed on the on-ramp, it slammed on the acceleration, putting the car's engine to use. Misty put the pedal to the medal and followed.

The two cars sped down the Shoreway, the Cleveland skyline in front of them, the dark lake to their left. Misty figured they knew they were being followed at this point, but she had a plan. She would follow them until they got off the highway and then she would try to make it look like they lost her. I was worth a shot.

Like two fighter jets in the sky, the Celica and the Honda Civic R Type weaved in and out of the slower moving vehicles, their engines blaring.

Misty stared straight ahead. A calm came over her. It was like the car was driving itself or like she and the car were one being. They reached downtown Cleveland, speeding past the Browns stadium and the glistening pyramid of the Rock and Roll Hall of Fame. Just then the Honda sped over to the exit lane and up onto E. 9th into downtown Cleveland.

The downtown area was unpopulated, as usual, so the chase continued. Misty followed the Honda into the Flats. The Flats were the low-lying banks of the Cuyahoga River, which had been used for industry before being converted into an entertainment destination in the 80's.

Misty drove slow, past the carefree people on the streets, running through the rain from one bar to another, screaming and laughing.

Both cars maneuvered stealthily through the crowds and down toward the Cuyahoga River.

The Honda stopped for a moment and Misty stopped a few hundred feet behind it. This was it. The Honda was about to get out. Were they operating out of the Flats? The area where all the bars and nightlife were? It would be a little obvious, wouldn't it? It was hard to imagine that a drug ring would be run directly out of a bar, but that's where they were and this was where the Honda had stopped and parked.

Misty put her car in park and turned off her lights. She sat, waiting for the dealer to get out of her car. She waited for what seemed like an eternity, breathing heavily from the adrenaline of the chase.

"I can wait here as long as it takes," Misty said to herself. "Won't be the first time I spent the night in the car."

Misty heard the loud bellow and turned her head to see an enormous 650 ft long barge. The blue lights scattered up and down its wet deck cast the barge in an eerie glow, its reflection rippling on the river beneath it. Misty was mesmerized by the industrial giant as it slowly crawled down the river, toward the lake.

Suddenly, the Honda Civic R Type turned on. It jetted out of its parking spot and back onto the road.

"Shit!" Misty yelled, fumbling with the keys to the Celica, aggressively turning them in the ignition.

The Honda sped down the hill, directly toward the Cuyahoga River. Misty followed behind, farther back, catching speed down the hill, trying to make up lost ground.

As the Honda sped over the bridge, a red light started flashing and a barrier came down, blocking the entrance to the bridge.

Misty slammed on the breaks. The road was slick and the Celica slid over the wet asphalt. Misty turned the wheel in an attempt to stop the speeding car before it slammed into the barrier. The car fishtailed and Misty screamed and braced herself for impact.

As it skidded to a stop, the rear of the car just gently nudged the barrier in front of the bridge.

Misty breathed a sigh of relief and looked up into the rearview mirror. Behind her, the bridge lifted and the barge passed underneath while the Honda Civic R Type sped up the hill on the other side of the river and out of sight.

CHAPTER FIFTEEN

-

THE NEXT MORNING, Misty opened Coffee Bucket and served the regular morning crowd. She was feeling defeated. She blew it, yet again. Here she had thought she was onto something and was getting somewhere, but as she saw the bridge lift she had sadly watched the blue headlights of her only lead fade into darkness.

She didn't have the energy to be upset about it. What was there to be upset about, when you no longer had even a frey of evidence to hold onto? Misty might as well have plunged the car into the Cuyahoga River, because she felt like she had been washed out into the lake and was just left bobbing in the darkness, waiting to sink to the bottom.

She wouldn't have done that, though, because then Gus would have known that she'd stolen his car for the night. If there was one thing Misty could have been proud of regarding her escapades from the night before, it was that she had returned Gus's car without having wrecked it in any way. There was a close call at the end, when she spun out as the bridge gate came down. But it didn't even leave a mark.

Misty had returned the keys to their hanging spot by the front door that night, while Gus was snoozing on the couch next to a couple 20 ounce cans of Budweiser. Easy. She didn't get that much sleep as she waited for the adrenaline to die down. She kept replaying every moment of the chase in her mind. Every intuitive turn of the wheel, every stealthy maneuver--never letting the car out of her sight. Until that final excruciating moment. She couldn't get the sight out of her head of the Honda smugly driving away victorious. She gritted her teeth and cursed into the night.

Tramaine seemed to be awake as well, with her curtain drawn and a dim light behind it, whispering on and on, about what Misty couldn't tell. It only made Misty feel more paranoid and more frustrated.

And now, at work, her lack of sleep was again catching up to her. She poured herself some coffee and took a sip.

"This shit is rancid," she said, before looking up and seeing her boss Summer standing in front of her. "Oh, sorry."

"Is that the new Brazilian blend? Yeah, I'm not a fan either. I'll order more Ethiopian for next week," Summer said as she unlocked the door to her office and went inside to put down her bags.

"Cool, cool, yeah, Ethiopian." Misty responded as she dumped six packets of sugar and four ounces of cream into her coffee.

Misty's plan was to just get through the shift and go directly back to the sober house for a nice long nap. Just get through the morning and then catch up on some sleep. Luckily, Summer was working and she was pretty good at picking up the slack. She just expected Misty to stay focused and do the work, which Misty was finding she actually didn't mind doing. She was getting the hang of the job, learning what tasks needed to be done when and helping customers quickly and efficiently. Summer didn't expect her to be overly friendly or anything and she let Misty just be herself, which Misty appreciated. She only got mad when Misty slacked off or was being lazy.

"This job is extremely easy, Misty," she'd say. "So, please just do it."

And when she put it that way, she really had a point. Misty was grateful for the job. She was able to afford to stay at the sober house and she even had a little money left over for Taco Bell and stuff. She was now receiving a weekly check and was in line to have a retirement plan.

The feeling of contentment was unusual for Misty and almost unsettling. She wasn't expecting to enjoy this job as much as she was. It only made the thought of having it taken away from her all the more treacherous.

The bell on the door jingled as it opened.

Misty watched as Detective Mills squeezed his fat ass through the front door, followed behind by two tall cops in full uniform.

"Well, well, well," Mills said. "How are we ladies this fine morning?"

"...fine, I guess?" Misty responded. "Can I help you with something?"

"Oh, I did come to pick something up, but it isn't coffee," Mills responded with a big grin.

He looked around the cafe, to see how many people were there, assessing just how loud he needed to speak. He raised his voice, just a touch to say, "I'm sure you're all wondering if we'd made any progress on the Cleveland Coffee Killer case."

Everyone kind of just stared at him, since, well, no one had asked, actually. But he continued anyway.

"I'm sure you, as coffee shop workers and coffee shop patrons have been concerned for your safety, of which it is our utmost concern as protectors of our citizenry." Mills smiled smugly. The two other officers stood behind him, menacingly, eyeing the people in the cafe, their faces stone cold.

"I'm happy to report that we have made significant progress in our search for the Cleveland Coffee Shop Killer."

The crown murmured with excitement. A few turned in their chairs to get a better look at the officer.

"We have, in fact, identified our primary suspect."

Misty's heart dropped. She stopped breathing. Her throat clenched up and time stood still. This was it. They'd figured her out. Did they identify her with the other local businesses she had made a scene in on the night of the murder? Was there some sort of video of her in the vicinity that night? Perhaps they had identified her car in front of Chevrolait after all. It didn't matter. She was screwed. She was too suspicious, she didn't have an alibi, she had a record and she hadn't found the real murderer, yet. This was it.

Detective Mills looked directly at Misty. His smile dropped.

"We identified our suspect and she works here," he added.

The people of the cafe audibly gasped. It was like the air was sucked out of the shop. Misty's eyes began to water. She felt like she was going to collapse. Her eyes darted around the cafe, looking for a possible escape route. She made the sign of the cross on her body and thanked the Lord for letting her get some ass at least once before getting arrested again.

"Summer Singh," Detective Mills stated, "you are under arrest. You have the right to remain silent. Anything you say can and will be used against you in a court of law."

Summer's eyes bugged out and her jaw dropped. "What!?" she screamed. "No!"

She fumbled for words as Mills continued to read her the Miranda rights. The other officers restrained her and put her in handcuffs. Misty was frozen. She didn't know what to do.

"Misty! It wasn't me! I didn't kill anyone! Misty, please!" Summer pleaded to Misty, her only life line at this moment. "I didn't do anything, I swear!"

Misty just watched, frozen as the officers led Summer out the front door. As the door jingled shut, the cafe burst into chatter as people pulled out their phones to relay the events to their friends and partners.

Misty just stood there, her heart pounding, her mouth dry.

The rest of the morning was a blur. Eventually, Mr. Larry showed up for his shift. Misty gave him the news.

"Summer? Arrested? Oh, dear," Mr. Larry said. "Poor girl. I do hope she didn't murder anyone and she can get out of this mess. Oh, this is awful. You kids really know how to keep me young, sweet Jesus Christ. If I wanted to deal with this mess I'd have gotten a job as a greeter at the Steelyard Walmart."

Misty biked home in a daze. Summer? Really? She did not want to believe Summer was the murderer. She'd already ruled her out as a suspect. But why? Just because she liked her? In truth, she didn't know where Summer was on the night of Vanessa's murder. She also didn't know where Summer was the night Jace was murdered. Summer had worked with both of them.

In Misty's eyes, the strongest case for Summer's innocence was that the dumb lug Detective Mills considered her the prime suspect. Misty just could not believe that Mills had the capacity to find the murderer before Misty did. He was the type that jumped to conclusions.

But isn't that what Misty had done? Jumped to the conclusion that Summer was innocent? All based on what evidence? Misty was going off her intuition, but Misty had watched enough television to know that intuition didn't hold up in a court of law. If Detective Mill was one step ahead of her, Misty would be pissed. But if Summer actually did do it, then it would actually be a relief.

Misty kept replaying the scene over again in her head. Summer's face as she was getting arrested. Her voice pleading, "I didn't kill anyone! Misty, Please!"

Misty stopped her bike and put her foot down. Her heart was pounding and her head was spinning. If she didn't figure this out soon it might haunt her forever. Of course Misty didn't want to go to jail, but she knew enough to know that she didn't want another innocent person to be there either. It almost felt worse.

"I'm going to talk to Summer. I'm going to find out what information she has. If she did do it, then maybe I'll be able to get it out of her. If she didn't do it, maybe she has a little more information that can lead me to whoever did do it."

Misty got back on her bike. She was so lost in daydreaming about all the possible scenarios that she had already locked up her bike before she realized all her worldly possessions were sitting in cardboard boxes on the front patio outside the sober house.

"What the fuck?"

CHAPTER SIXTEEN

-

Misty burst into the sober house, furious.

"Who touched my stuff!"

"AAHHHHHHH!" came a horrified scream from the living room.

Tramaine was sitting with her arm around Joan who was curled up into a ball on the couch.

"What the hell, Misty?" came Chelsea's raspy smoker's voice from the kitchen. She came into the room with a steaming warm towel. "Thanks a lot!"

"Who touched my stuff. Why are my things outside?" Misty stood there, confused and angry.

"You're kicked out, bitch!" Chelsea said as she placed the warm towel on Joan's forehead.

Joan dry heaved over a bucket, her body convulsing uncomfortably.

"Kicked out?"

Tramaine traded spots with Chelsea, who took her job holding onto Joan as she writhed with discomfort. Misty noticed a pleasant aroma from the kitchen.

"Is someone baking," she asked as Tramaine approached her.

Tramaine looked extremely serious, deathly serious, as she motioned for Misty to join her outside.

"What the hell, Misty?" She asked, disappointed and angry.

"You tell me, Tramaine. Why is my shit out here?"

"You don't know what's going on?"

"No!" Misty shouted.

Tramaine rolled her eyes.

"You can't smell anything?"

"It smells like cinnamon rolls or something."

"Is that all?" Tramaine asked.

Misty sniffed the air. She moved toward the door to sniff some more.

"Did I clog the toilet, again?"

"You brought drugs into the sober house, Misty. You think we weren't going to find your weed inside a toilet paper roll? Are you stupid?"

Misty's heart sank. She had totally forgotten. And she was stupid.

"Joan is in there suffering from reefer madness. She found it almost instantaneously this morning and she couldn't resist. I woke up and she had already baked cinnamon rolls, two pans of cookies, a pecan pie and biscuits and gravy. I'm pretty sure she's stoned out of her mind and now she's having hot flashes."

"Oh, my God," Misty said. "From weed?"

"Yes!" Tramaine shouted. "This isn't a joke, Misty! We live in this house because we are sober! And we're sober because we need to be! Maybe some people can just smoke weed and go on with their lives, but not Joan. One puff of the ganja and she loses all sense of herself. She may have to go to a recovery center."

Misty felt terrible. She felt like she was about to dry heave.

"I had no idea."

"Well, you should get a clue," Tramaine said. "You put all of us at risk by bringing drugs in here. I ignored you coming home smelling like stale beer the other night--giving you the benefit of the doubt. But this is too far. You have to go. Now."

Tramaine went back inside. Misty heard the door lock behind her. She could hear Joan crying inside and Tramaine comforting her and Chelsea's raspy voice shouting, "Fuck this!"

Misty stared at her possessions sitting on the ground in front of the house. A box of toiletries, some of her grandma's old knick-knacks and a pile of clothes: pajama pants, t-shirts, flip flops. It wasn't much, but Misty wasn't sure how she was going to transport it all on her bike.

She marched up to Gus's house and pounded on the door.

"Helloooooo?" she called out. "Gus! I need to borrow a car for real this time!"

Gus was inside, leaning along the doorframe between the kitchen and living room, his arms folded.

"Yeah, I don't think so, Misty," he responded. "You made a mistake."

"I know I made a mistake. I get it, I can't stay here anymore. But I can't take my things around on a bike."

"You can leave them here until you find a way to transport them. Or just move them one by one on the bus or something," he said casually. "Where there's a will there's a way."

"You are such an asshole," Misty replied. She left the back door and snuck around to the front. She tiptoed up onto the front porch and peeked inside the front door. She could hear Gus fumbling around, still in the back kitchen. She creeped open the door and felt her hand around on the wall inside, looking for some car keys. Quietly she removed some from the hook.

She slowly closed the door and turned around. Gus was standing at the bottom of the porch staring at her.

"You think you're smooth, huh?" he asked. "Yeah, you got away with it one time, but you think I'm gonna let you steal my car again?"

"I didn't steal your car!"

"Just because you returned it, doesn't mean you didn't steal it. What were you doing, going for a joyride in the rain?"

"Shut up. I didn't do shit."

"You got caught, Misty."

"You never drive the Celica anyway!"

"Exactly, that's why I thought it was strange that the ground underneath my Celica was wet from the rain. It would be dry under there if it hadn't been moved. Nice try, babe. You stole your landlord's car and then brought drugs into the sober house. You know you think you'd have a little more respect for the people that offered you a place to stay, but maybe some things never change. You just care about yourself."

"You should talk! Taking advantage of drug addicts while you drink PBR's in your house and the government writes you a check. I know what kind of scam you're running this time, Gus! Sad that they let just anyone run a sober house these days."

"Well, the only complaints I've gotten from my tenants are about the chick who brought drugs into the house, so the only person who has a problem with my scam is actually you."

"FUCK OFF!" Misty screamed. She huffed off down the street in a rage. "You suck! You all suck! You don't even know anything about me! A bunch of BULLSHIT! FUCK!"

Strangers peered out of their windows at the crazy lady in the Tweety Bird t-shirt screaming on the street.

The door of the bus opened and Misty stared at the front steps of the Justice Center before her.

"Hurry up, lady, I got a schedule to keep," said the bus driver, urging Misty to get off the bus.

Misty turned around and flicked him off. "I've got arthritis in my knees! Asshole!" Misty lied, as she pretended to struggle off the bus, wincing audibly. "Ahh. My knees. Old good-for-nothing bones. Ahh, my old bones." She took her time to the last step, then jumped off, turned and flipped off the driver again. "Suck it, homie!"

In reality, Misty didn't want to get off the bus. The Department of Corrections was the last place that Misty wanted to be. It was the very place she was trying so hard to avoid ending up. But she had scheduled a visit with Summer. For some reason, Misty believed Summer. She didn't think that Summer was the murderer. For one thing, she didn't really have a strong motive. Was a $2.50 raise enough to murder for? Also, she stood up for Misty when Detective Mills was on her ass those first few days of work. If Summer was the killer, why not let Misty take the blame when Detective Mills was being hard on her?

It was hard for her to believe Summer was capable or interested in murdering someone in cold blood. But as Misty sat behind the bulletproof glass and listened to Summer explain the situation, she began to second guess her own instincts.

"Listen, Misty, I didn't do it. But they have a lot more on me than I anticipated. For one thing, they know that I went on a date with Jace. Apparently he told some of his coworkers."

"Okay," Misty replied. That was some drama. Vanessa and Jace had dated and then Summer went on a date with Jace. "Why didn't you tell me?"

"I didn't think it was a big deal. It wasn't a relationship or anything," Summer added. "It was one date."

"Okay," Misty said. "But it doesn't prove you killed anyone. What else did they say?"

"Well," Summer took a deep breath, then quietly added, "my gun was found in a dumpster behind Jace's apartment, where he was killed."

Misty was shocked. "Excuse me? Your gun?"

"One of my guns," Summer clarified.

"Summer, you have multiple guns?"

Summer nodded.

"What the fuck," Misty said, putting her head in her hands and looking down. She was confused. She didn't expect Summer to be a gun owner. The other day, when Summer asked if Misty wanted a gun, she thought she was just joking. "Whyyyy?"

Summer stared off into nothingness. It was silly. It had started when she needed to pick up some essential items. Paper towels, a lightbulb, athletic socks, a shower curtain liner and hemorrhoid wipes. She needed to take a trip to Walmart. The Steelyard Commons Walmart.

The Steelyard Commons was one of the most stressful places in Cleveland. A huge shopping plaza located next to the steel mill, it had everything from Target, to Home Depot, to Panda Express and another Aldi. It was usually teeming with people from all over the city.

The Walmart was a free-for-all. Items were scattered about, misplaced and disorganized. However, it was the closest place to where

Summer lived and she wanted to get the shopping trip over as quickly as she could.

She popped a Xanax and made her way to the Steelyard. Two hours later, Summer was leaving the store with paper towels, athletic socks, color-changing LED lightbulbs, 2 handguns, a hunting rifle and a silencer.

"Fuck," Misty said.

"I don't know what got into me..." Summer shook her head. "I mean, there was the Xanax. That got into me...and then the sporting goods employee, Brad, made it sound so necessary and simple and it was just so easy that it felt like I had to get one. And I was on Xanax. And don't get me wrong, I was just as surprised as you when it wore off and I realized what I had done."

Misty was shocked. She didn't know someone could accidentally buy three guns.

"And a silencer," Summer added, cringing. "I kept them at home for a few days, but I didn't feel safe with them there. There's a closet with a combination lock in the office at Coffee Bucket, where we keep the safe, so I decided to keep them here for a little bit. It made sense to me to keep them there because they'd be behind lock and key and I figured I was more likely to get assaulted or robbed at work than at home. It... it made sense to me at the time."

"But if they were locked up at the office, how did the murderer get the guns?" Misty wondered out loud. "If the murderer wasn't you that is."

"Misty! It wasn't me!" Summer wailed desperately. "Apparently, someone got into the closet and took the gun. I don't know when, because I never really check if the guns are there or not. But whoever it was didn't take any money from the safe, because that I would have noticed. They just took the gun."

Misty tried to piece it all together. Summer had worked with both the victims. The victims had dated each other and Summer had also slept with one of them. Both victims are dead. One was found dead at Summer's workplace and the other was likely killed with one of Summer's guns, which was found at the scene of the crime.

"This looks really bad, Summer," Misty said.

Summer shook her head and looked Misty directly in the eyes.

"I didn't kill anyone. I swear."

Misty knew the feeling. Misty had spent every day since she discovered the body preparing herself for the fate that Summer may be suffering, assuming she hadn't done it.

"Misty," Summer said, quietly. "This is gonna sound so stupid and pathetic, but... will you feed my fish for me?" Summer's face began to melt and tears streamed out of her eyes.

"Yeah, yeah. Sure. I can do that." Misty had never been able to keep a fish alive before, but she figured maybe if they were someone else's fish, she'd be better at it.

"Thanks, Misty. There's a spare set of keys under the flower pot on the porch. You can stay there if you want," Summer added. "I bet Julian and Fred would appreciate the company."

"Your roommates?" Misty asked.

"No, my fish!" Summer smiled.

Misty wasn't happy about it, but she was extremely relieved at how a new apartment had just fallen into her lap, albeit at her friend's expense. She would finally be able to relax all by herself. She began to wonder how much a new vibrator cost.

"Time's up, ladies," the guard said from behind the glass.

"Please help me, Misty," Summer pleaded. "They looked up my hoo ha and anus with a flashlight when I got here."

"Those fuckers. Okay. Where were you the night of Vanessa's murder?" Misty rushed.

"With Jace."

"Where were you the night of Jace's murder?"

"By myself at home."

"Shit," Misty said.

"Please believe me, Misty," Summer asked. "I can tell my lawyer doesn't."

Misty paused. She closed her eyes and took a deep breath. She looked at Summer behind the glass in her orange jumpsuit.

"I believe you," Misty said. "Someone broke into your office and stole your gun. That is some bullshit to do that. But it narrows our search. Whoever it was had to have been in your office before. They had to know the guns were there. I'll be back and we can talk about it more. Just hang in there, we'll get you out of this."

Summer looked at Misty with wet, foggy eyes.

"Thank you, Misty," she said as the guard grabbed her arm to take her back to her cell.

CHAPTER SEVENTEEN

-

MISTY CRACKED OPEN A BUDWEISER and put her feet up on Summer's coffee table.

Julian and Fred were feasting on food flakes and the setting sun was casting an orange glow on Summer's charming little apartment. Though her belongings were still piled up near the front door, Misty already felt at home.

Luckily, Summer also lived pretty close to Coffee Bucket, so Misty was able to walk her things from the sober house to where Summer lived in only a few trips.

Misty yawned and extended her arms out over her head, resting them on the back of the couch. She admired Summer's apartment. It was cozy and comfortable and maintained the eclectic style that Summer displayed in her dress. A fish skeleton sat amongst the plants on the shelves. An assortment of lamps adorned one cluttered corner of the room while an enormous bean bag chair occupied another.

Misty got up and stared at the fish for a while. She opened and closed the fridge a few times, unsatisfied with the oranges and kombuchas she found in there.

"Where's the freaking TV?" she asked out loud. "Another ho without a TV? Who are these people?"

Eventually, she started digging through her things until she came across a roll of toilet paper.

"Toilet paper?" she said. She then noticed a plastic baggie stuffed inside the roll. "Oh shit! Those bitches didn't even confiscate the goods! Hell yeah!"

She ran to the corner store and got herself some rolling papers, a handle of Tito's, a 2-liter of Sprite and a dozen eggs, which she would use to egg Gus's house if she got drunk enough.

Summer didn't have a TV, but where one should have been, there was a record player. Luckily, Misty had lived with her grandma long enough to know how to operate one, so she slipped on one of Summer's Prince records to help get the party going.

Misty was drunk and doing what she did best, snooping. Who was Summer? Misty had based her innocence off of nothing more than her intuition. She wandered the apartment looking for more clues, anything that would make Summer seem suspicious.

The apartment was tidy enough. It wasn't filthy and full of trash like the kind of apartment an unhinged psychopath might live in. But it also wasn't the kind of meticulously clean, untouched maintenance that a control-freak serial killer might uphold.

The apartment was honestly really cute. Summer had plants and fish, all of which were alive, which Misty considered in Summer's favor. Misty went back in the kitchen. It was painted a light peach color and the windows were decorated with curtains that had a white and blue geometric pattern on them. Decorations were hung along the wall above the small kitchen table, signs that read "Bless this Mess" and "Live Love Laugh" and "My Kitchen, My Rules."

Misty felt welcome and comfortable. Would someone who had something to hide invite Misty to stay at her place? Misty noticed a calendar on the wall in the kitchen. Every month had a different picture of a classic car on it. Misty took it off the wall.

There's gotta be something in here.

Misty set her High Life down on the kitchen table and placed her joint on a saucer. She scanned the last month of dates. Summer had written down when certain bill payments were due, a doctor's appointment, therapist appointments, family birthdays and when her period started. Then, on September 17 was written "meeting J & V. 8pm."

Misty finished her beer and cracked open another one. She took out the rolling papers and began to roll herself a joint.

"All right, now..."

So now the three of them were up to something together. Misty wondered what it could be. Did they have a threesome? Would Summer have mentioned that to her during their conversation? Would you write a threesome down on your calendar? What could they have been meeting about? Maybe it was a work thing? When did Jace stop working at Coffee Bucket? Whatever it was, Misty needed to find out what that meeting was about.

Misty felt good. She flipped over the Prince album to the B-Side. Misty was feeling jazzed and she was ready to get stoned.

"Damn it!"

Misty realized she hadn't bought a lighter.

"Summer's got to have a lighter in here, somewhere. All these freaking candles..."

Misty rummaged through the kitchen drawers and the drawers in the coffee table. Eventually, she made her way into the bedroom. There was a candle on the bedside table. She opened the bedside table drawer. She saw a pink lighter. As she grabbed it, she noticed a small white envelope with some writing on it. She picked up the envelope and drew it closer to read the scribbles.

"See you when i get off - J"

Misty held the envelope up in front of the bedside lamp. Inside was the silhouette of a house key.

Misty smiled a disgusting drunk smile.

"Time to take a bike ride," she said to herself.

Misty wondered if she should swing by the sober house one more time on her way to break into Jace's apartment. She went into the kitchen to grab something out of the refrigerator.

But the eggs never found the vinyl siding of the sober house or the flaking painted wood of Gus's front porch.

The farthest the eggs got was the concrete sidewalk just outside of Summer's apartment building, where they lay smashed, next to a pair of empty flip flops as the door of a windowless white van slammed shut and sped away.

CHAPTER EIGHTEEN

-

When Misty opened her eyes, it was dark. She felt something around her head. When she tried to remove it, she couldn't move her hands. They were tied together behind her back.

"Kinky," she tried to say, but she was gagged and couldn't do anything more than moan.

She was in a moving vehicle. It had a certain smell to it, slightly rotten and musty, with a hint of patchouli and cedar. She heard a soft, muffled voice.

"Pull in here."

Misty's body leaned into someone next to her as the car took a sharp turn, eventually pulling to a stop. The van door slid open and Misty felt hands in her armpits, directing her to the door and pushing her out. She didn't mind the assistance helping her walk--she was still drunk from the case of beer and vodka she'd been slamming.

Misty's hands were still tied behind her back and her head still hooded when she was placed in a hard metal chair. The room felt humid and there were some light humming sounds and again, a familiar smell.

"He'll be here soon," she heard another voice say.

Misty wiggled and squirmed. She tried to find a weakness in the ties on her hands, but they were secured tight. It was quiet in the room, aside from the mechanical humming, Misty's metal chair clanking around and a few muffled giggles of people laughing at Misty while she tried to free herself.

Eventually a door creaked open and Misty heard the sound of expensive loafers clicking on concrete.

A white, middle-aged man's voice spoke from the other side of the large room.

"We know you've been investigating Vanessa Bergeron's death. We know you've been snooping around the Cleveland Hydroponics facility. We know you were at Chevrolait the day Jace was killed. And we know you tailed a drug dealer. Unsuccessfully."

Misty tried to object to the accusations, but she was wearing a mask and was still gagged, so she just ended up with a lot of drool running down her face. She twisted and struggled in the chair until the voice finally spoke up.

"Go ahead. Remove the mask."

After a moment of whispering, the mask came off and Misty's eyes adjusted.

She was in a large warehouse. She could see her shadow long before her. Behind her, it was quite bright but in front of her it was darker. She could see stacks of what appeared to be mattresses lined up along the wall to her left. To the right were the warehouse doors, which remained closed. In front of her it was darker, but light shone on a large desk with a suited man behind it.

Misty let her eyes adjust. She squinted to get a better look at the man. He was flanked on either side by a large man and a large intimidating woman. They wore sunglasses and crossed their arms.

"Are you working with the police?" He asked. His voice sounded oddly familiar.

"Eew! No!"

"It's an honest question."

"Do I look like a fucking pig? You act like you know so much about me and then you ask a bitch question like that. Jesus."

"We know enough to know that you're desperate. We know enough to know that you could be blackmailed into working with them. It's an honest question considering your recent behavior."

Misty rolled her eyes. They landed on the mattresses stacked against the wall. She looked back down at the man behind the desk and squinted. Mattresses?

"Wait one second. Dick Vagantis?" She said. "Dick Vagantis Cleveland Mattress? Holy shit! It's Dick Vagina! You know, you look shorter in person."

Misty knew she'd seen that face before. It was Dick Vagantis, the owner of Dick Vagantis Cleveland Mattress. She'd seen him on billboards and on TV commercials since she was a kid. She and her cousins used to call him Dick Vagina.

"Why did I get kidnapped by the Vagina Mattress guy?" Misty asked, looking around. She could tell there were people behind her. She tried to turn around, hoping someone would give her an answer. "I'm confused--why does the mattress guy care about Vanessa?"

"I don't care about Vanessa. I care about my business."

"Mattresses?"

"Hah. No."

Misty looked around again for answers. She finally got a glimpse of the person behind her. It was the drug dealer she had tried to follow.

"Marijuana."

"Yeah. You got it. In addition to being Northeast Ohio's #1 mattress retailer, I also happen to be the kingpin of the west side's marijuana economy."

"Well that explains the dank smell in here. I thought that was just me. Good stuff!"

"Thank you. The mattress industry has changed. Kids are buying mattresses online and off of podcasts and whatnot. It hasn't been easy to keep up and, well, I've had to diversify my business, albeit underground, but nevertheless."

"And Vanessa was working for you, underground."

"We had a strong business relationship. I liked Vanessa. I even gave her a mattress."

"So then why would you kill her? Was she going to out you?"

"Out us for staying underground? How well did you know Vanessa?"

Misty recalled her conversation with Grover, the anarchist. She remembered him talking about Vanessa preferring things to be underground.

"I knew Vanessa well, but I don't know you well. I know Vanessa liked working on the black market."

"She did. She did," Vagantis nodded his head. "I never had to question Vanessa's loyalty and she did great work for me. Listen, I don't know what exactly you're doing, snooping around like you are, but I'm going to need you to stay out of my business. That means I don't want you coming around here anymore. I don't want you contacting my dealers. And I don't want you anywhere near Cleveland Aquaponics. Got it?"

Misty squinted. "Cleveland Aquaponics? What do they have to do with any of this?"

"Just stay out of it and we won't have any issues."

"What if I want to get some compost and wall veggies?"

"Get them somewhere else! Whatever it is you're trying to do, it's not going to work out. The best thing for you to do right now is stop what you're doing. Stop snooping and just enjoy your stupid little life."

"You enjoy your stupid life! Don't tell me what to do!" Misty did not like being told what to do.

"Listen, lady, this can go one of two ways. Either you mind your own business or we make your business our business. And trust me, I take my business seriously. Do they give you health insurance at that little coffee shop? Because if you make a bad choice, you may end up needing it."

"Shut up. It's a free country."

"You ever had six mattresses accidentally drop on top of you? It's not a pretty picture."

"I've had two drop on me and it wasn't that bad!"

"Well then I guess we'll have to figure something else out. Why don't I introduce you to my two finest employees. Crazy Sword, Numb Nuts, you have any ideas?"

The two thugs standing on either side of Dick Vagantis stepped forward. One pulled out a crazy sword and the other a pair of nunchucks.

"What the hell? Is this another Dungeons and Dragons group? I can't handle this," Misty was pissed.

"Take her outside. Teach her a lesson." Dick Vagantis got up and left the room.

Misty already felt like she was going to blow chunks from all the alcohol. But now she was about to get roughed up. And unfortunately the effects of the liquor were wearing off. Chances are she was going to feel every little bit of this. One of the thugs poked Misty with their nunchucks to get her up out of the chair.

"I'm moving, I'm moving. Yeesh," Misty said.

Her head was spinning from standing up and as she turned around, the brightness of the lights behind her was blinding. As they led her out the door, her eyes focused up and she was able to see row upon row of marijuana plants, all growing vertically in walls that looked extremely familiar, right down to the fine blue mesh on the back of the system.

It was dark outside. Misty was shoved to the ground.

"We can fuck her up now or we can fuck her up later, after she fucks around and keeps snooping," said the thug with the nunchucks. "Me, personally, I like to get it out of the way, now. What do you think, Crazy Sword?"

"Well, Numb Nuts, normally, I like to wait. Give them a chance to do the right thing," replied the thug with the sword. "But something about this bitch makes me think it might be better to just get it out of the way, let her know exactly why she doesn't want to snoop around anymore."

Crazy Sword scraped his sword on the ground, making an upsetting sound.

Misty's head pounded as she sat on the cold hard ground. She was deciding how much of a fight she was willing to put up. She laid herself down on her back.

Just kill me already, she thought.

Her head was spinning. Her stomach was churning. Her ears were ringing.

"Who's that?" Crazy Sword asked.

"Who's what?" Numb Nuts responded.

The ringing in Misty's ears got louder. And closer? Laying on her back, she arched her spine and tilted her head backwards, looking behind her, the world upside down. Two headlights were speeding toward her.

"Someone's going to steal your kill," she said to the thugs, not even bothering to brace herself for impact.

The car sped towards them and then suddenly began to spin out. Crazy Sword and Numb Nuts jumped out of the way, expecting the car to crash over Misty and into them. But the car perfectly spun to a stop right in front of where Misty was laying down. The passenger door popped open.

"Get in."

Dust coated Misty's face, but through the fog in her eyes Misty could see the popped up headlights of the gold 1988 Toyota Celica blinding Crazy Sword and Numb Nuts, who held their weapons in front of their faces, shielding their eyes.

"Hurry the fuck up!" Gus shouted.

Misty scrambled to her feet and hopped in the car. Gus started speeding away before Misty could even close the door. As she finally slammed it shut, she heard the grinding of Crazy Sword's weapon scraping against the gold metal of the automobile.

Misty shouted at Gus through the cold night air as it blew through the open windows, her heart racing.

"I thought you were going to run me over!"

"You like that?" Gus shouted back. "I call it the jackknife!"

CHAPTER NINETEEN

-

The golden Celica sat parked in a lot overlooking the twinkling glow of the industrial valley. Smoke stacks shot smoke and flame into the air, trucks rumbled along transporting rubble and molten steel, the aroma of toxic farts filled the air.

"I work down there," Gus said. "Union job. Pays well. And I get to drive a huge truck."

Misty was silent.

"Get to transport stuff. Steel. Fuel. Pretty good job."

Misty just sat there.

"Anything you want to talk about?" Gus asked.

"No," Misty said, flatly.

Gus thought about his next question.

"Do you--"

Misty cut him off.

"I didn't ask you to come save me, by the way."

"Sure, sure," Gus said. "But when I opened that door you jumped up and got your ass off the ground like it bit you or something."

Misty tried not to grin, imagining what she looked like.

"How's the damage look?" Misty asked, referring to the side of the car that had been sliced open with a katana.

"It's bad. Real bad. But nothing I can't fix," Gus stared out over the valley, thinking about all the ways he could repair his baby.

"So, how did you know where I was? Were you following me?"

Misty asked.

"I had a nice talk with the girls at the house."

Misty rolled her eyes and mumbled, "Bitches."

"They wanted me to look out for you," Gus said. "And Tramaine had a lot to tell me. First of all, apparently Joan never smoked any of your weed, so there was no chemical relapse."

"I figured. I found it all in my stuff. Smoked a bunch of it earlier."

"But Joan smelled it and had some vivid flashbacks. Apparently she is highly sensitive to smell. Which is why she's always cooking nice things."

"And why you had to install that high velocity exhaust fan in the bathroom."

"Oh, no, that was because of you. All the girls asked for that after you moved in."

"Oh." Misty grimaced.

"Joan is embarrassed about how she reacted. But, you know, everyone's entitled to a dramatic episode every once in a while. God knows we've had ours, girl."

Misty shook her head. She'd rather not recall her and Gus's episodes.

"But it was still a big mistake to bring drugs into the house, Misty."

"I know," she admitted. "It was an accident."

"That's what Tramaine told me. She told me you've been snooping around about your co-worker's death and that you were planning on tailing a drug dealer to find out more information and that the weed was probably from that and you probably weren't even thinking when you brought it back to the house."

"I wasn't!"

"I believe that," Gus said. "So, after our talk I decided to find you and invite you back to the house. I knew you were staying at Summer's because I followed you to see where you were taking all your shit. But when I went to ring your buzzer I stepped in some eggs. I looked down and saw your nasty-ass flip flops."

"Sorry I wasn't wearing my best kicks when I got kidnapped,"

Misty said sarcastically.

"I knew something was up, so I rushed back to the house. Luckily, Chelsea knows every drug dealer in the city, so she clued us into the fact that there is really only one place where west side weed is coming from: the Dick Vigantis Mattress warehouse. It was a shot in the dark, but with the girls' help, I found you."

"I still hate all of you. And I'm still staying at Summer's. At least until I get her out of jail."

"Do you want to break her out?" Gus asked, sincerely.

"No," Misty said. "No. She's innocent, but I want her out because I got the right one in."

Misty felt around in her pocket. She gripped the key tight in her hand.

"I need you to drop me off somewhere," she said.

"All right," Gus replied. His hand went to his car key to turn the ignition. But Misty's hand stopped him.

"In a minute." Misty stared at Gus. Her other hand delicately caressed his rat tail.

The Celica rocked back and forth, its windows full of fog. The wild howls, loud fleshy slaps and screams of pure ecstasy coming from the car faded right in with the hum and rumble of the machines in the valley down below.

The next morning at the coffee shop Misty's heart sank as she remembered that Summer wouldn't be there with her. Misty was dying to tell Summer that she hooked up with her ex last night, but the only people in the coffee shop were Mr. Larry and Jeff and Jerry, retirement guys.

"All right, Mr. Larry. Just sign here, initial here and sign here and we're almost halfway through," Jeff said, while the elder Jerry watched on to make sure everything was being done correctly.

"See how easy it is, Mr. Larry? Just a little paperwork and now the company is going to match your retirement and you're on your way to earning free money. It's that simple," Jerry added. Misty looked over and noticed that Jerry was staring at her deliberately while he said this.

Misty wished she could tell him that she had been kidnapped last night while investigating the murder of two former baristas in an attempt to free herself and her friend from suspicion, so maybe his retirement thing was the first thing on her mind at the moment, but she decided to keep her mouth shut.

"Sorry, Mr. Larry, I don't mean to be rude. I'm just beginning to worry that Misty doesn't like us," Jerry added while Jeff quietly continued to direct Mr. Larry through his paperwork.

Mr. Larry looked up and smiled. "Oh, all the customers think that when they meet Misty. But don't worry about her, she's a peanut. Her shell's not that hard to crack."

Misty gave Mr. Larry a grin and returned to her work stocking the fridge. Her mind wasn't focused on the retirement plan or whether the customers liked her or not. She was still replaying the rest of her night.

After Gus dropped her off she snuck back out. Dick Vagantis had warned her not to snoop around, but nunchucks or no nunchucks, Misty wasn't going to let the vagina mattress guy order her around. She took her key to Jace's apartment and went around to the back stairs. His apartment was on the third floor.

As she reached the top floor of the back porch, she noticed the caution tape. A tape outline of Jace's body was still on the wood planks.

"So he was murdered outside his apartment," Misty thought to herself.

Whoever it was murdered Jace outside the apartment. That's risky. If Summer had a key to Jace's apartment, why would she murder him outside the apartment? It would be easier to ambush him inside his apartment and there would be fewer risks of anyone seeing or hearing it.

Misty stepped carefully under the crime scene tape and tiptoed through the crime scene to the back door. It was still locked. She took out her key and slowly let herself in.

She turned on a lightswitch and the apartment lit up with an ambient glow. Misty walked through the kitchen into the living room. It was beautifully furnished in a very cool, masculine style. Several dim lamps throughout the room illuminated the leather couch, wood furniture and maps and artwork on the walls, which were painted a rich blue. One wall was lined with bookshelves, on which sat many books, some plants and other trinkets. On the coffee table was a nice ashtray with cigarette and cigar butts on it. A glass and metal rolling bar was stocked with scotch and gin.

She turned around and returned to the kitchen. The floor was sparkling. Misty looked closer and realized it was broken glass. The window above the sink was broken. So, the murderer had tried to get into the apartment, after all.

Misty continued to make her way through the apartment looking for evidence. The bedroom was boring, aside for some butt plugs she found in the closet. She recalled Jace's big old booty and felt relieved that he was giving his ass the pleasure it deserved.

The second bedroom was converted into an office. Taped to the top of the desk were a bunch of index cards with handwritten motivational messages on them.

"Don't wish for it, work for it."

"Become the hardest working person you know."

"If you want to go fast, go alone. If you want to go far, go together."

"Do not follow where the path may lead. Go instead where there is no path and leave a trail."

"There is no fear, it's all just a perception."

"Coming together is a beginning; keeping together is progress; working together is success."

"A leader is one who knows the way, goes the way and shows the way."

Misty thought the whole thing was kind of psychotic. She had to make a motivational vision board in court-ordered group therapy once. She ended up just cutting out pictures of hot bodybuilders from a Muscle and Fitness magazine, pasting them into one big orgy.

Jace was competitive and motivated, Misty knew that. It's why she took him as a suspect before he himself was murdered. He was an obvious social climber. It's possible that his motivation and competitive nature got him in trouble. She checked the cigarette butts for weed, wondering if maybe he was involved with Dick Vagantis, as well, but they were just American Spirits, no marijuana to be found. Also, Vagantis never mentioned Jace, only Vanessa.

Misty opened the long drawer underneath the desk. Inside was a manila folder labeled "Project U."

Misty opened it up. The top page was a spreadsheet listing "Employees." The sheet listed names and marked whether each name was "on board," "interested," "neutral," "not interested" and "against." It reminded Misty of the survey she'd filled out at the library.

Jace and Vanessa's names topped the list with both marked off as "on board." Summer's name was listed and marked as "not interested."

There was an assortment of other names and a column listed as "location." A majority of the names were marked as "on board" or "interested." Still others were marked as "neutral," "not interested" or "against."

Misty had been up all night with adrenaline, but back in the coffee shop, the high was wearing off. Misty poured herself a cup of coffee and stared at it. Jace's folder was now sitting on the kitchen table at Summer's apartment and Misty was dying to get back to it so she could look through the rest of the documents inside. Anything that linked Summer and the two murder victims was evidence.

Her shift was almost over and she had plans for after work. She impatiently watched the clock, getting ready to leave.

"Thanks for coming in early to fill out the paperwork, Mr. Larry," Jeff said pleasantly. "Misty, would you like to stay after to fill out yours?"

Misty cringed. They already clocked her for slacking on this, but Misty couldn't stay after--she had a bone to pick with the anarchists. Their relationship with Dick Vagantis went deeper than Grover had let on and it had almost gotten Misty killed.

"Sorry, I have plans after work and I'm kind of tired. I think I'm gonna take a coffee to go and finish up here," Misty said.

Larry grabbed a to-go cup and poured it for Misty. "Four creams and six sugars?" he asked.

Misty nodded.

"I know how you like it," he said with a smile as Misty went to the back room to grab her things to leave.

Mr. Larry brought Misty her coffee.

"Here you go, Misty. And don't let those guys out there give you a hard time. You're special just the way you are. Have a lovely afternoon, Peanut. See you tomorrow," he added, sweetly.

Misty headed outside to her bike. As she approached it she noticed a piece of paper attached to her handlebars, flapping in the cool autumn breeze.

Misty grabbed the paper and opened it. Written in thick black ink and sloppy, demented handwriting was a message:

"Leave town or you're next. Sincerely, The Cleveland Coffee Killer."

CHAPTER TWENTY

—

"I HAVE A DRUG KINGPIN CHASING ME with nunchucks at night and the Cleveland Coffee Killer threatening my life in the morning," Misty said to herself as she biked down the street. "I must be doing something right."

Misty knew she was taking a risk when she went and looked at Jace's apartment the same night she was kidnapped. But she estimated that she could sneak in there before Vagantis had the opportunity to have someone follow her.

However, Misty wanted to take more precautions when returning to the Cleveland Aquaponics facility, which Vagantis seemed particularly obsessed with.

She already thought it was strange that the weed kingpin knew about her asking questions at Cleveland Aquaponics. What wasn't clear was why that was threatening to him. Why would it matter to him that Misty was learning about vegetable walls? Misty wanted to find out, but she didn't want to draw too much attention to herself. She was going to need some help.

Misty hesitated before lightly knocking on the door of the sober house. No one answered. She knocked a little harder, waited about two seconds and began to walk away.

"Hello?"

Misty heard Tramaine's voice from the door behind her and turned around.

"Hi, Misty," Tramaine said.

"Hi, Tramaine."

"What's up?"

Misty looked at the ground.

"I'm sorry I brought that dank smelly weed in the house. I wasn't thinking," Misty said. Misty hated apologizing, so she kind of sounded mad while doing it.

"I understand. Thank you for apologizing. It caused a lot of trouble for us and really threw Joan into a fit. And the rules of the sober house are the rules and we have to be strict about them. For a lot of us, being sober is crucial to us being able to live, so I hope you understand why we had to kick you out."

"I get it," Misty kicked at some gravel. She didn't want to hurt anyone. She was just caught up in her own world. She wasn't really thinking about the girls at the house and she felt bad about that.

Tramaine went back inside and returned with a batch of cookies. She offered one to Misty, who took a bite and then shoved the whole thing in her mouth.

"Gus said you found a place to stay?" Tramaine asked.

"Yep," Misty replied, pieces of cookie flying everywhere. "It's not too far from here. Pretty nice place. Furnished apartment. Kind of smells like fish food but it'll do."

"So what's up, did you leave something here?"

"Nah. I just... I think I need your help."

An hour later, Misty emerged from the sober house looking fierce in a pink faux suede fringe cropped jacket, a sexy white crop top pleated blouse and high waisted bright blue denim that hugged her thighs with intentional rips where her sexy skin peaked out. She even had on faux snakeskin knee high boots with a chunky heel. She had on full coverage make-up with a strong contour and a smokey eye and on her head was one of Tramaine's finest wigs: a wavy maroon highlighted lace front that went just past her shoulders.

Considering most people had only ever seen Misty in pajama pants and Cedar Point souvenir t-shirts, it was a pretty convincing disguise.

"Now don't get any food on that stuff, Misty. I want it back in perfect condition."

Misty tried her best to walk around in her new look.

"I feel like a ho."

Tramaine put her arm gently on Misty's back to help steady her.

"You look like a ho," she said proudly. "You look like a sexy ass bitch who knows what she wants and is gonna do whatever it takes to get it. But you've always looked like that to me."

Misty looked into Tramaine's eyes and felt warm.

"Tramaine?" she asked. "I can trust you, right?"

Tramaine looked a little offended.

"Of course, Misty. Why do you think you couldn't trust me?"

"Well, I caught you whispering in the middle of the night a few times. Are you hiding something?"

"Oh, my gosh," She said. She looked a little embarrassed. "Misty... I haven't told you what I do for work, yet, have I?"

"I guess I never asked..."

"I stream ASMR on Twitch," she said. "Basically, I whisper into the microphone and people watch me. I don't tell a lot of people about it, but it's a good living. I pretend to be a nurse or a teacher and people pay me money to do it."

Misty recalled her first suspect, Bart at NubCorp. He said he was making money screaming while playing games online. Now, here was Tramaine pretending to be a soft-spoken doctor on the same website.

"Thanks for telling me that," Misty said. "It kind of freaked me out waking up to that night after night."

Tramaine ordered Misty a car and instructed it to drop Misty off two blocks away from the Cleveland Aquaponics facility. When she was done she was to go to Cheryll's Automotive Repair a few blocks away and use their phone to call Tramaine. Tramaine was friends with Cheryll and she knew Misty would be stopping by.

Misty got out of the Lyft and began her walk to the aquaponics facility. Every car that sat parked on the side of the road looked suspicious to her. Every car that was driving too slowly made Misty worry that it was someone looking for her.

It was a colder day, now in late autumn, so the garage door to the warehouse was closed. Misty approached the large metal door that was the entrance to the facility. It had a sign on it that said, "Come on in," with a smiley face image on it.

Walking into the facility, the smell hit her almost instantly. It was the same slightly rotten, musty smell with a taste of cedar and patchouli.

Grover, Michelle and Big Ben were all in their respective locations: Grover in the workshop area, tinkering with his designs, Michelle in the office hovering over her laptop and Big Ben rolling around barefoot in slop.

Misty approached Grover slowly... and sensually, in her new outfit. She flipped her hair and said in a soft, airy voice, "I have an appointment for a tour."

Grover stopped what he was doing. He looked up at Misty and was visibly shocked by what he saw.

"We aren't giving tours currently," he said, his brow furrowed with confusion. "Did she seriously schedule a tour? We're not supposed to be giving tours." Grover sounded frustrated.

Misty looked around and said quietly, "It's me. Misty."

"Who?"

"Misty Cheevis. I was friends with Vanessa..." Misty said. She inhaled deeply and was about to start making orgasm sounds to remind him, but he interrupted her.

"Oh! Oh, yes. That's right. You probably shouldn't be here, Misty."

"I'm not here. Champagne is here. I don't know who Misty is," she said, trying awkwardly to wink her large false eyelashes.

"Come on. Let's go upstairs." Grover got up from his drafting table and led Misty to the staircase in the back.

Upstairs Misty took off her wig. She was sweating like a pig. Grover went to the kitchen and poured her a glass of Miller High Life.

Misty chugged the High Life. She was panting and out of breath.

"What's going on?" he asked, handing her the glass. "You shouldn't be here. Detective Mills stopped by here the other day. He asked us about you."

"What!" Misty choked on her High Life and started coughing. "Did you tell him anything?"

"Of course I did! What was I supposed to do? Lie?"

"Yes! I thought you were an antichrist--I mean anarchist!"

Grover blushed. "Let's just hurry up and get this over with. Why did you need to come by here?"

"Dick Vagantis told me to stay away from you. Why? All you said was that Vanessa was involved in drugs, you didn't mention that you and your aquadingdongs were up to some shit too."

"I don't know what you did, but you pissed off Vagantis. He's not happy."

"What I did? He kidnapped my ass and tried to slice me into sushi! I'm just trying to find out answers and it doesn't help when people like you lie to me! How do you know Dick Vagantis? What the hell does vegetable walls have to do with mattresses? Clue me in!"

"Dick Vagantis funded our aquaponics company under the table with weed money. He gave it directly to us and we started it, but we still owe him money. It's not a good situation. He's been on our ass for months now. He made us diversify the business and add composting and watering plants in offices to our services. We were worried he had a hit on Vanessa to threaten us or something."

"Vanessa didn't work for you, though. How would killing her threaten you?"

"I don't know, exactly! But when we heard she'd been killed we worried about ourselves. We knew she was working with him and that he was unhappy with us! Give us a break! We're still not sure her death doesn't involve us, to be honest. We're trying to figure it out, too. But let's just say Dick Vagantis isn't the most open communicator."

"What other reasons would Dick Vagantis have to kill Vanessa that don't involve you? After you introduced them, she must have formed her own relationship with him, right?"

"I can't say for sure. She seemed to be working closely with Vagantis. She told us he was trying to move his weed operation above ground. Medical cannabis is becoming legal in Ohio and he wants to get in on that. But it's very exclusive. Apparently he's been freaking out about the transition. Investigators could have a problem with his success on the black market and it could compromise his ability to sell medical. It's a shady situation and Vanessa said it was causing him and his business a lot of stress. He was extremely paranoid. It might explain why he was bothered by you snooping around."

"Yeah, he seems stressed and a little bit defensive. Did he think I was an investigator or something?"

"Maybe. You kind of ask a lot of questions."

Don't remind me, Misty thought. Her head was spinning and her eyes were having trouble focusing. She felt like she was going to barf, but it also seemed like her body was somehow resisting it. Her heart was pounding like she'd just finished an intense game of laser tag.

"Maybe Vanessa was going to snitch and rat him out for being an illegal business?" Misty suggested.

"I don't think so. Vanessa preferred working on the black market. She was a true blue anarchist. She hated the government and she hated taxes. She didn't want Vagantis to transition his business. She was more likely to try to convince him to keep selling illegally. And from what I understand, she was having a lot of success selling weed underground. There's a possibility her own success in the drug business put a target on her back."

"So you owe Vagantis money, huh?" Misty's head was spinning. She tried to change the subject.

"We owe him a lot."

"Well, your vegetable walls sure are growing him a lot of weed." Misty's mouth was filling up with spit. "His warehouse is full of them. Could you sell him more of those?"

"What?" Grover looked extremely confused. "He hasn't bought any vegetable walls."

Misty wanted to argue, but she couldn't form any words. Her vision was becoming narrow as darkness reduced her vision to a pinpoint. She just nodded and stared at Grover.

"Misty what are you talking about? Are you okay? We never sold any aquaponics to Dick Vagantis."

Misty was getting angry. Grover was accusing her of lying. But she didn't have the energy to argue or even focus.

"Blue... mesh..." was all she could say before her face went white, her eyes rolled back into her head and Misty collapsed onto Grover's organic hand woven Tibetan area rug.

CHAPTER TWENTY-ONE

-

THE FLUORESCENT LIGHTS OF THE HOSPITAL ROOM were harsh as Misty groggily regained consciousness.

Misty sighed as she took in her surroundings. The patient gown on her body, the IV in her arm and Judge Judy playing on the TV up in the corner of the room.

"This is some bullshit," Misty said out loud. "How the hell am I going to afford this bullshit. Fuck!"

She screamed the last bit rather loudly, causing her nurse to run in the room.

"Oh, you're awake!" The nurse said. "Is everything okay? Do you need anything, miss?"

"I need out of here," Misty said.

"We'll get you out of here as soon as possible. I'll be right back," the nurse said, removing herself from the room. One episode of Judge Judy later she returned. She wasn't alone.

"I called you as soon as she woke up," the nurse said as Detective Mills entered the room.

He grinned.

"Misty," he said.

This was the last person Misty wanted to see in her hospital room. She felt vulnerable and trapped, strapped in by the IV and medical devices surrounding her.

"What happened?" he asked.

"Like I fucking know?" Misty snapped. "Ask Nurse Betty. Fuck."

"We're still trying to figure out exactly why she lost consciousness. She has a whole range of issues: high blood pressure, high cholesterol, dehydration, fever, obesity, eczema, hemorrhoids and low blood sugar, she might have lupus and I think she's menopausal. When's the last time you saw a doctor, hun?"

Misty just stared at her, angrily. The nurse continued to speak to Detective Mills..

"On top of that, she fell extremely hard when she fainted. It's likely she has a concussion."

"Concussion?" Misty said. "So? I've had four of those already. It's not a big deal."

"I'll leave you two alone," the nurse said as she carefully walked around Detective Mills' huge badonkadonk and out into the hospital hallway.

"Thank you," Mills said, while not breaking his creepy gaze from Misty.

"I have hemorrhoids, too," Mills said.

Misty was repulsed, as usual. Mills was disgusting. She just wanted him to go away.

"So, you dressed up like a hooker to take a trip to the local anarchist hang-out where you chugged a beer and passed out, Misty. Care to explain?"

"It's none of your business."

"Except that Vanessa worked at Coffee Bucket and she was involved in a book club at the Aquaponics Facility and you are the only other link between the two organizations. Therefore, as the lead investigator in Vanessa's death... I guess it is my business, sweetheart."

Misty did not want to deal with this.

"You know, we already arrested the Cleveland Coffee Killer, Misty. Yeah, she's already locked up. So maybe you can stop playing Sherlock Holmes or whatever you've been doing and go back to your home for recovering drug addicts. Nice crowd you run with."

"You have the wrong person. I got a letter from the Coffee Killer today. It told me to leave town or I'm next. It was taped to my bike. Not sure how the killer would write that from jail, but whatever."

"Or maybe you wrote it and taped it to your bike. I know you visited Ms. Summer in jail. Whatever plan you came up with to prove her innocence isn't going to work. You can walk up three flights of stairs in whore high heels and pass out all you want, but unless you or another barista turns up dead, Misty, the Coffee Killer has been caught and my job is done."

"Good plan. Just wait for another person to die. Solid plan, chief."

"Coming from the person who is forging letters in order to interfere with a criminal investigation, that's rich. Your friend is going to prison, Misty. And for a long time. Her hearing is coming up and we're pushing for a quadruple life sentence."

"Quadruple life sentence? Is that even possible? She's killed two people max--that doesn't sound right."

"I don't know, sweetheart. I'm a detective, not a lawyer. But, trust this, if you continue with your shenanigans, you're going to be spending a little more time with your friend than you anticipated. In prison. Although, you probably won't end up at the same prison. But you'll both be in prison, is kind of what I'm getting at."

"Yah, I got it."

"And when this is all over, I'm gonna be on the front page of the news, holding your friend's head on a silver platter, eating hors d'oeuvres of another silver platter that doesn't have a head on it, at a huge party in my honor when I'm named Chief of Police as a reward for my success."

Detective Mills made his way to the door and turned back before he walked out.

"Take care, Misty. Get well soon. But not too soon. I like you better when you're bedridden."

CHAPTER TWENTY-TWO

-

Misty checked out of the hospital. When they handed her the clothes she arrived in, Tramaine's clothes, Misty asked if she could borrow some masking tape so she could just close up the open back of the hospital gown and wear that out instead.

Misty sat in her hospital gown and stared out the window at the muggy grey skies over Cleveland. Almost nothing was going through her head. She couldn't even muster the strength to scowl. She just kept saying "Fuck," over and over again in her head and sometimes out loud. She said it with disdain, she said it matter-of-factly and she said it with an air of desperation and sadness. "Fuck."

Walking up the stairs of Summer's apartment building she just kept saying out loud, "This sucks. This sucks. This SUCKS! FUCK!" The sounds echoed through the stairwell. It was demented.

Back in the apartment, Misty stared at Jace's folder on the kitchen table. She felt tired and decided to just take a shower, scream a little bit and then pass out naked in Summer's bed. She had work the next day and she had already missed work the day before when she was in the hospital, so she was going to have to explain that, too--something she wasn't looking forward to.

The next day she rolled up to the front of the coffee shop. On the door was a sign, printed on white paper.

"We're sorry to inform you that Coffee Bucket will be closing. Thank you to our customers for the memories!"

"What?" Misty said out loud. "Closed? Fuck!"

Misty was out of a paycheck. She slammed her hands on the front window and pounded on them. Screaming and pounding like King Kong.

Suddenly the front door opened.

"Misty?"

It was Mr. Larry. He was inside packing up the store. He invited Misty in for a cup of coffee.

"Do we have any Sprite?" Misty asked. She was sick of coffee. She never even liked it in the first place. Fuck coffee.

"From what they told me," Mr. Larry explained, "business wasn't doing that well before the Coffee Killer, but after the initial bump of interest after the killing, most people were turned off by the murder and business dropped again. Not to mention, the owner of the company was apparently living in Arizona, siphoning money off the top and leaving the business in major debt. Upper management tried to get a loan to buy the business from the owner, but they couldn't find a bank that would give them the funding, so everyone agreed to just close up shop."

"I didn't agree to it!" Misty yelled.

"Neither did, I!" Mr. Larry said. "I thought we were doing a fine job!"

"We were fucking awesome! I even made a heart design in a cappuccino once by accident!"

"And I just figured out how to change the settings on the iPad so the letters are big enough for me to read it! Oh, you got a phone call, by the way. I took a message. Someone named Grover. Like on Sesame Street!" Mr. Larry said.

Misty called the number using the shop phone. Grover told her to meet them at the facility.

"You can just dress normal this time," Grover added, the image of Misty falling over in her stilettos and smacking her head on the ground replaying in his head.

Grover and Big Ben were waiting for Misty at the entrance to the facility. They led her to the meeting room where Michelle was waiting with a smile on her face. She handed Misty a bottle of water.

"Anyone else?" Michelle asked, brightly.

The facility had the usual familiar smell to it, which left Misty feeling tense. It reminded her of the time she was almost killed in a mattress warehouse.

"What's up," Misty asked. She was ready for this meeting or whatever to start.

"Well," said Grover, after a heavy sigh, "we have some information to share with you."

"Like how you were working with the guy who kidnapped me? A little late, don't you think?"

"I'm sorry about that, Misty. I really am. I didn't expect him to kidnap you. But... you mentioned... before you passed out..." Grover and Michelle looked at each other and kind of cringed. "Before you passed out you mentioned that Dick Vagantis had aquaponics at his facility. Specifically, my aquaponics design."

"Did I say that?"

"You did. We found that to be disturbing, since I have a patent on my design and we never sold him our product or agreed to let him use them."

"Okay, so?"

Michelle took over. "We looked into your claims and discovered that Dick Vagantis is using our stolen wall system. And to great effect. Nearly his entire operation is run using our low cost, low waste aquaponics system. Even more low-cost since he never paid for the product."

"So he stole it?"

"Yep," Michelle said, nodding. "We confronted him, but he admitted nothing."

"Here's our theory," Grover said, seriously. "Vanessa spent a lot of time here at the facility. We believe that she stole the mesh irrigation systems and the wall designs and sold them to Vagantis. Or possibly he paid her to do so. Our guess is that with the plant walls in his hands, he needed to tie up loose ends and that's why he offed Vanessa. Either that, or Vanessa threatened to blackmail him and he chose to murder her before she could release any damaging information about him and his drug ring.

Misty sat there, taking it all in.

So, according to the Cleveland Aquaponics crew, Vanessa worked for Dick Vagantis and stole the plans and stuff and then he killed her for some reason.

"Wow," Misty said. "And he admitted to that?"

"No," Grover said. "We don't have any concrete evidence or proof. But, that's where our heads are at, now. All we know for sure is that we never sold him a plant wall, we never sold him the patented mesh we use to build them and we never sold him the blueprints for our specific wall design. Yet, somehow, his facility is full of our walls."

"But do we have proof that he killed Vanessa?" Misty had one goal and one goal only: find the killer who was now sending her death threats.

Michelle and Grover shook their heads. Misty felt a rage bubbling up inside of her.

"Then how does that help me? Or Summer?"

Grover, Michelle and Big Ben were confused. They didn't know who Summer was and they didn't understand how closely Misty was involved--that she started this whole investigation. It was vital for her to find concrete evidence of who did it. She had to prove it. With evidence. Not just guessing that Vanessa stole something and then maybe the guy she stole it for got mad. Misty didn't care about green walls and blue prints or whatever. All she cared about justice, whatever color that was!

Misty was getting visibly heated and the anarchist aquaponics people were getting uncomfortable. Big Ben excused himself.

"I have to turn the compost," he said before leaving the meeting room to continue his work, his bare feet slapping on the concrete floor.

"Listen, Misty. We want justice for Vanessa just as much as you do, but if Dick Vagantis had her killed, it's going to be really hard to enact justice on a prominent businessman and crime lord. That's just the way it is."

Misty was pissed and breathing heavily. She suddenly got a whiff of a pleasant aroma.

"What's that smell?" she asked. "It smells like flowers."

Michelle smiled. "Oh," she said. "That's my perfume. It's Dior."

"Did you just put it on?" Misty asked.

"No. Not since this morning. It's Dior. It lasts like all day. I barely have to put any on because it's just such high quality. It'll last me forever and it's the kind of perfume I feel like I could wear until I'm 80. It's timeless without being dated, you know?"

Michelle went on about Dior, comparing it to Chanel and Lanvin. Misty wasn't listening. She shook her head. Something wasn't right.

Misty had discovered one crime: the theft of the aquaponics technology. But she could care less about intellectual property. She was interested in murder. And she had one more piece of evidence to look at.

Misty's least favorite thing in the world after running was reading. She didn't understand how anyone could find enjoyment in reading books or whatever. She remembers having to read out loud in school and all the kids laughing at her.

She stared at the folder sitting in front of her, praying that whatever was inside was easy to understand and written at a third grade reading level, max.

Vanessa wasn't the only one dead, here. Jace had been killed, too, and the aquaponics fools never mentioned Jace being involved with Dick Vagantis' operation.

In the mind of the Aquaponics trio, the murder was about them. It was about their technology. But Misty wasn't convinced.

Misty looked over the paper in front of her. Here, the two victims and the person stuck innocently in jail were all linked. But what was this paper about? What were Vanessa and Jace on board with that Summer was not interested in.

Just fifteen seconds of looking at the diagram and Misty had to get up and walk away. Trying to comprehend this bullshit was giving her a hernia.

She called the county jail to see if she could get a face-to-face with Summer. Maybe Summer could explain this to her, considering her name is on it. Unfortunately, they couldn't get her in for another two days. Misty scheduled the appointment, but she needed to understand this and she needed to understand it now.

She showed the materials to Tramaine. After looking them over, Tramaine suggested they talk to Dungeon Master Theo. He had a better understanding of anarchist politics and could maybe explain what was going on in the folder.

The first item of evidence Theo was drawn to were some personal statements written by Vanessa and Jace.

Vanessa's read:

"There is enough to share. We just choose not to for whatever "reasons" AKA EXCUSES! We choose to let people hoard resources while others suffer and die for lack of resources because of [excuses]. Excuses that incidentally amount to white supremacy, but excuses nonetheless. There is a solution. SHARE RESOURCES! It is a choice not to solve these problems and I am not okay with it. I AM REALLY NOT OKAY WITH IT!"

Misty's eyes bugged out. "What the fuck is she talking about? That bitch was crazy."

Theo tried to offer an explanation.

"Vanessa believed the world could be different and she thought it was simple. For her, it was easy to see a different world, to see past the excuses. What was hard for her was understanding how other people couldn't see past them."

Tramaine nodded. "She seemed to think that if we just shared resources, everything would be fine."

"Sharing resources? Are you sure she wasn't talking about Settlers of Catan?"

"I don't think so," Theo said, looking over more of the documents stuck into the folder.

Jace's statement was full of weird narcissistic personal ambition tied up with some social justice themes.

"What is success if not success for the benefit of all? Greed and imbalanced power structures have gotten in my way and prevented me from succeeding to the extent that I should based on the hard work, knowledge and passion I possess for my craft. True success requires me to take on a leadership role in providing a course correction within my industry. I believe in taking things into my own hands. May the best man win."

Theo shared his theory.

"It's clear to me that Vanessa and Jace were likely trying to drum up support for a barista union. According to this spreadsheet, no single cafe had strong majority support for a union among its baristas. However, there was strong interest among many throughout the coffee shops they had apparently spoken with. They could have been trying to form a union across the different cafes."

Theo looked closer at the chart.

"Based on how this chart looks, I wonder if they have actually spoken to everyone, or if some of these positions are based on presumptions from other baristas they had spoken to. Either way, it's risky business to be drumming up support for collective bargaining. It's likely that those in the business who have established power won't want to give it up to a union. That's just the facts. It would be like just giving away all the wheat you've been hoarding and a handful of your victory points, just because the other players asked you to. To continue the Settlers analogy."

"Don't use that analogy, please. That game makes no sense to me and it actually just sucks," Misty scowled. "If making a union is risky then why even do it? And is it really worth killing someone over?"

"Possibly. Being in a union would give the employees more say in how the business operates. For example, they could decide they want the company to provide them healthcare or other benefits. They could also intervene to raise wages and improve working conditions. It's a threat to the owners, because it means that the union might decide the owner shouldn't be getting as much money. Furthermore, it would be more than just an economic move; it would be a political one."

"So you're saying one of the cafe owners or something could have killed them to stop them from interfering with their bag," Tramaine noted.

"Maybe, but based on this chart, it doesn't look like they were having that much success. So, I don't know. If you're the owner, why not just find a reason to fire them?" Theo asked. "I don't know exactly what was going on, but they were definitely causing trouble. I mean, it's the right kind of trouble, but it is the kind of trouble that some people might be very threatened by. I'm proud of them," Theo had a glimmer in his eye.

Misty walked home with Tramaine. The ground was littered with leaves and the air was crisp. Tramaine was trying to follow where Misty was going.

"Okay, so the aquaponics people think that Dick Vagantis had Vanessa killed because she knew about the stolen blueprints or whatever, right?"

"Right," Misty said.

"And this folder of union stuff gives us reason to believe that maybe someone high up at the coffee shop had them killed in order to prevent them from forming a barista union."

"I guess," Misty conceded.

"What do you think?" Tramaine asked.

Misty thought for a moment.

"Bitch..." she said. She didn't want to think about it anymore. She took a deep breath. "If it was about the aquatopics walls why would they kill Jace? If it was about the union, why threaten me? I'm not joining a union. And they closed the coffee shop! It doesn't even exist anymore."

Misty walked Tramaine home and then continued down the tree-lined street back to Summer's apartment. Dark clouds painted the sky and wet leaves littered the ground.

Misty was feeling hopeless. She'd just lost her source of income and after all this time, her investigation hadn't helped her close in on the killer. In fact, it had opened her eyes to the possibility that the murderer could be hidden by the world of organized crime or high politics. It seemed like maybe this wasn't as simple as a crime of passion. The idea that Misty could somehow track down the killer and ensure justice seemed foolish and naive. She felt like an idiot for ever thinking that she could do such a thing.

She remembered when she was stalking her previous employer at Pizza Fever., she thought she'd done something good, discovering his theft of company money. But he was engaged to the owners' daughter and so instead of punishing him, the punishment came down on Misty for bringing the issue to light.

The world wasn't fair. The world belonged to the people who ran shit.

Misty started to investigate Vanessa's murder so that she wouldn't end up in jail. Sure, this time the hammer didn't come down on her, but it had cracked down on Summer, and Misty felt like it was somehow her fault. She remembered the look in Summer's eyes when Misty had agreed to try to help her out--the glimmer of hope.

It pained Misty to think how stupid it was for either of them to believe that she had the power to do anything.

"I'm just a loser without a job, crashing at my incarcerated friend's apartment," Misty thought to herself. "Nothing has changed."

She stood there on the street as the sky grew dark and the tall street lights flickered on.

CHAPTER TWENTY-THREE

—

Misty spent the next couple days getting high and drinking. She couldn't fathom having to find another job. She slept, masturbated and got wasted. She figured she deserved a reward for having found herself a job and place to live at least once. It was overdue for her to have some kind of celebration. And celebrating her past success was a good enough excuse for her to justify not finding a new job.

After a few days, Misty returned to the jail to meet with Summer. She showed her the information from Jace's house.

"Oh, yeah. They tried to get me to be in a union or something. They said it would require everyone to be on board and working together and stuff and to be honest, I just didn't think that would ever happen. I took that job so I could just go to work, do my stuff and go home. I wasn't looking for any drama or big fights or to change the world. My theory was to just find something that worked and be grateful for it, so I told them I wasn't interested."

"Do you think anyone from Coffee Bucket would murder Vanessa and Jace for making a union?"

"I have no idea," Summer replied. "The sporting goods employee at Walmart told me that you really never know who could be a stark raving mad lunatic psycho killer and obviously I was convinced!"

Misty understood. Whoever was the killer seemed to have gotten away with it. She stared at Summer, sitting behind bulletproof glass in front of her.

"We're never getting you out of here. This sucks. It's so stupid. I'm probably gonna end up in there, too, if the detective has his way."

"I figured if they went through the trouble of framing me, it might be hard to find out who it was," Summer said, calmly. "They definitely caught me off guard."

Misty left the jail with a sinking feeling in her stomach and a lump in her throat. It wasn't fair. It wasn't fair to Summer or Vanessa and it wasn't fair to her that it would end up like this. Despite knowing that she was stupid and that there was no reasonable likelihood that she could figure out who murdered Vanessa, Misty still felt like she could do it. Feeling her own genuine belief in herself, despite any logical reason to do so, only made Misty feel all the more naive.

Misty stopped at a few different coffee shops on the way home to see if they were hiring. Some asked her for a resume, which she still didn't have, and others were already having trouble finding hours for the baristas they'd hired.

At Chevrolait, Misty sat at the counter and asked for a hot chocolate. After the barista asked her how her day was going, Misty explained how she'd spent the day searching for work, to no avail.

"Have you tried Super Coffee?" the barista asked.

"What's Super Coffee?" Misty asked.

"Super Coffee Coffee Drive Thru," she continued. "It's their third location. They're opening up just off the Interstate 71 Bellaire Road exit. They're expecting a lot of traffic. It's probably a more fast paced environment. Not your typical lazy coffee shop lifestyle, but it's a job. Also, the owners are assholes and Republicans. And they make you wear a futuristic silver tubetop."

The barista let Misty use their phone in order to call and set up an interview. Apparently they were desperate for baristas who had both a working knowledge of espresso machines and the ability to tolerate a low hourly wage, likelihood of fewer tips given the drive-thru nature of the shop and, of course, the humiliating uniforms.

None of this was a problem for Misty, for whom humiliation was a driving life force.

"Alrighty," said Bert Kelley, the retail manager of the Super Coffee Coffee Drive Thru restaurants. "Now that you've signed the form that lists all the things we can fire you for: forgetting to put whip cream on drinks, forgetting to say 'Have a Super Coffee Day' with every drink, etc. We now just need you to sign up for the retirement plan and we will be on our way!"

Misty rolled her eyes. Here we fucking go.

"Where's the pen?" she asked.

She was meeting him at the corporate offices in Independence, near where she had visited BJ, the former Coffee Bucket employee, at his new job at NubCorp AccessLink SysTech.

"You don't want to hear about the plan? I can have Jeff and Jerry go over it with you later this week, if you'd like," Bert Kelley said with lackluster, bureaucratic enthusiasm. "But it is mandatory for all employees."

"Yah, yah. Jeff, Jerry, whatever. I get it. Let's just get it over with. Where do I sign?" Misty asked.

"Ah, now there's a smart employee," Bert said, handing her the contract and a pen. "It's free money. Sign here. Other employees are skeptical of it--oh, what's the catch? Initial here. They can't just accept that free money is free money and we'll match it. Sign here. Everyone's always got a problem with something: long hours, initial here, fewer tips, initial here, silver lame uniforms, initial here, mandatory retirement plan, initial here. You can't win! And here. And here. And here. Sign here. And we're done! Welcome to Super Coffee Coffee Drive Thru. I have you closing tomorrow--don't be late."

Bert walked her to the door and slammed it behind her leaving Misty alone in the grey hallway under the fluorescent lights next to a large tropical plant. She wondered if Grover was the person who came by to water it every week.

Another shitty job. Yippee.

Misty wasn't feeling thrilled. There was some relief that she wouldn't be without an income. Summer had paid rent for the current month, but Misty agreed to cover it for the rest of the lease. So she was happy to have income for that purpose. Also, Misty had grown attached to the fish and they were really picky eaters.

Misty showed up at the sober house that night for a family dinner. Tramaine wanted her to reconnect with Joan and Chelsea to help smooth things over from the drama that ensued after Misty brought home weed.

Chelsea met Misty at the door. She sniffed Misty up and down, searching for even the faintest smell of marijuana.

"She's clear," Chelsea called back into the sober house.

Dinner was awkward, but without too much drama. Misty apologized to Joan and thanked Chelsea for helping Gus find her when she got kidnapped. Afterwards they worked on a horse puzzle and listened to Frank Sinatra for a little bit.

As she was leaving, Tramaine pulled Misty aside and handed her some mail.

"There's something from the hospital in there," she said.

Misty looked down at the envelope with the Lutheran Hospital letterhead in the corner.

"Fuck," she said. "Hospital bill. Let's see what the damage is."

Misty slowly opened the envelope. There was a paper inside, but she didn't see any dollar signs on it. It wasn't a bill. The letter was a "toxicology report" and included in it was a note from the doctor.

"The patient's sample contained a high concentration of dimethyl benzyl ammonium chloride, commonly known as Steramine, a disinfectant used in restaurants and food service."

"What the hell does that mean?" Misty said.

"That's the little blue sanitizing tablets you use at Coffee Bucket," Tramaine said as she looked over the report. "Misty, it means you were poisoned."

CHAPTER TWENTY-FOUR

-

POISONED?

Not only was Summer not the Cleveland Coffee Killer--she couldn't have poisoned Misty from jail--but the Cleveland Coffee Killer was still hard at work. And trying to kill Misty!

Misty's head was spinning and her thoughts were running around in circles.

Whoever poisoned her had to have access to something she was eating or drinking. And why? Was she being targeted for investigating the murders? But she wasn't even getting close! Or maybe she was closer than she thought.

Whoever the killer was, they had access to Summer's office in order to get the guns and had access to Misty's beverage, in order to poison it.

Misty's head was spinning. The more she thought about who it could be, the dizzier she got.

Tramaine and the girls offered to let Misty stay at the sober house for the night. Gus decided to stand guard at the entrance with his shotgun overnight.

"I don't need anyone to guard me," Misty said.

"Girl, someone tried to kill you. How do you know they aren't gonna come get you again." Tramaine was looking for weapons in the kitchen drawers.

Joan had pulled the drapes closed tight and Chelsea changed into something sexy.

"Is the killer coming here? If I'm going to die tonight, I need to look cute."

"You look like you're going to offer the killer some inexpensive personal attention," Joan countered.

"Or that! Whatever it takes! I don't want to die! Bob's Falafel House needs me!"

Misty needed some time alone. Maybe if she was by herself she could get her thoughts straight.

"I'm gonna stay at Summer's tonight, guys. I'll be fine. I can take care of myself."

"Like hell you can!" Gus said as he spat tobacco into an empty can of Schlitz. "We have a better chance of ambushing them here in my backyard. I'm gonna set up some barbed wire bunkers and I got some smoke bombs we can use saved up from my trip to Michigan."

"Whatever," Misty said. "I'm gonna take as shower."

Misty let the water run and the bathroom steam up. She sat on the toilet. She ended up taking a pretty long, big shit.

"I don't freaking get it," she thought. "Fucking steramine?"

Misty couldn't get to sleep. Tramaine offered to whisper her to sleep for free, but Misty told her to stop being such a creep.

Misty just stared at the ceiling. As she lay in her bed and the hours passed, images swirled across the ceiling.

Vanessa's body in the dumpster. The note on her bike. The broken window at Jace's apartment. Her grandma's wrecked car. Summer's office closet full of guns. Walls of mattresses. Walls of marjuana. And Steramine. The fucking disinfectant they used at Coffee Bucket.

Eventually Misty drifted off. She fell into a deep sleep and didn't wake up until late the next morning.

When she awoke she was in a trance. What she had dreamt was unlikely and unusual and strange, but it also made a weird kind of sense. She felt half in her dream and half on earth as she prepared for her first day of work.

Gus insisted on dropping Misty off at her new job.

Super Coffee Coffee Drive-Thru was a space-aged themed coffee shop. Located just next to the off ramp of a major highway, this third location was a circular building with a tall pointed roof in the center, topped with a shiny spire. Two lanes went around the side, where customers could place their coffee orders. The other side of the building had parking spots where customers could receive carside service from baristas on rollerskates.

Misty was dressed in her uniform: her belly peeking out of her silver lamé tube top and a cute little sailor cap on her head. Tramaine thought Misty would look cute with a blonde-ponytail attachment, but Misty declined the offer. Misty's booty put the shiny booty shorts to the test and the gym socks sat wrinkled around her ankles since they wouldn't fit around her calves.

The manager Tiff showed Misty around quickly.

"We're understaffed and the drive-thru is already out of control. I've been told you have coffee experience so I expect you to jump right in. For the time being we won't be doing carside service until we can hire more people--maybe some teenagers. I opened this morning, so I have to leave at one, legally. But you'll have some help closing. This is Mr. Larry and he'll be here with you until close at 8pm."

Mr. Larry winked at Misty from the drive-thru window where he stood with a headset as he blended a white chocolate frappa-dappa-doo.

After that, there wasn't much else to the day besides making drinks as fast as possible, cleaning up the inevitable messes that happened and wasting time trying to find which cabinet and drawer held the necessary supplies.

Overall, Misty didn't really mind it. With no indoor dining room, there were fewer dishes and virtually no stupid chit-chat with boring customers.

Every once in a while, she was able to fit in a little time with Mr. Larry between customers.

"Looks like they were pretty desperate to hire people," Mr. Larry said. "How do I look?"

What was supposed to be a tight, silver tank top hung loose on Mr. Larry's skinny little body. His white hair puffed out underneath a headband that had two springs with plastic coffee cups on top of them, bouncing around.

"Yeah," Misty said. "It's funny how demanding they are when they obviously need to hire people. I just agreed to everything, because I gotta have a job!"

"Me, too," Mr. Larry agreed. "But I'm thinking once I start I can probably get away with not doing some of the stuff. I still haven't signed the retirement plan," he added. "I'm elderly, Misty. What good is a retirement plan going to do me?"

A horn honked and Misty and Mr. Larry had to get right back to work. For the most part Misty was completely zoned out for the rest of the shift, just ringing people out and handing them their drinks. She and Mr. Larry made a good team. Soon enough, the sun set and the line began to dwindle down until eventually Mr. Larry switched off the glowing "Open" sign out front.

"That's that!" he said.

As they cleaned up the cafe and prepared it for the morning, Misty could tell Mr. Larry was slowing down. Misty made a phone call and shortly after a car pulled up around the front of the building.

"I called you a car," she said to Mr. Larry. "I can take out the trash and close up."

"Oh, Misty, you didn't have to do that," Mr. Larry said.

"Don't worry about it," Misty said as she walked him to the door and wished him a good night.

Misty finished up in the cafe, mopped and piled the trash by the back door.

She took a deep breath. Well, here we go, she thought.

It was dark outside. A solitary streetlight shone over the parking long. There wasn't much else around, besides a dark vacant shopping plaza adjacent to Super Coffee. Cars continued to zoom by on the interstate below.

Misty hauled the heavy trash to a large dumpster.

"Where's the old man?" said a voice.

"Well, so much for the two-for-one special. I guess we'll have to settle for just one," added another voice.

Two dark figures were silhouetted by the streetlight.

"Hi, Misty."

"Retirement's come early."

CHAPTER TWENTY-FIVE

-

"It's free money!"

Jerry's phone rang at 11pm on a brisk night in mid-October.

"We got 100 percent participation at Coffee Bucket. That should put us over the top. Best in the region, congratulations."

"Jeff?" Jerry said, sleepily.

"See you tomorrow. Don't spend your bonus all in one place."

Jerry looked at his phone. The call had ended.

Jeff had called Jerry while on his way home from having dragged a boxcutter through the thin skin under Vanessa Bergeron's chin, before shoving her dead body in a dumpster behind Coffee Bucket as a solitary muffin rolled toward the open back door of the cafe.

Best in the region, he thought as he drove through the darkness. The bonus is ours.

Jeff had started at Simbiox Asset Management a few months earlier. It should have been a good fit for him. Jeff was excellent with numbers. He knew calculations and could see patterns and strategies before anyone else.

However, in the line of business he was placed, it didn't matter what the numbers said. He was trying to sell retirement to people like Vanessa. Smug baristas, careless about their futures. If he didn't have to deal with them, Jeff would easily be first in the region—maybe even the country.

"I'm just not interested," she'd say when he'd ask to discuss the retirement plan with her.

"Not interested?" Jeff couldn't understand. "It's free money!" he'd scream after he and Jerry politely left the Coffee Shop and got to their car. "What is wrong with these people? What's wrong with them!?"

"Let me tell you about people," Jerry responded. "I know people. And can you stop slamming your fists on my dashboard, please?"

Jerry was a family man. He was raised in a traditional household in the Cleveland suburbs. He went to Ohio State University to get his degree. Met a woman to call his wife. Her dad got him a job at Simbiox Asset Management. They started a family. Bought a house. Ended up with five children.

Jerry was a salesman. Numbers weren't his weapon; charm was. He could talk to anyone. Or so he thought. He could sell retirement to anyone, so long as they were gainfully employed in a comfortable office setting. But Simbiox was looking to aggressively expand their retirement program and now Jerry was expected to sell to the weirdos and freaks working strange hours behind counters, over stoves and on shopping mall sales floors. His charm was lost on these people.

"People don't know what's best for them. They're suspicious. They think anyone trying to help them is going to scam them. But to be honest, I'm more surprised with these business owners. We offer the owners themselves a cut of the investment if they help us get 100 percent participation within their company. If I were them, I'd just make it mandatory company policy. Easy peasy. These employees would be better off for it. You can't expect a drive-thru worker to make good decisions."

Jeff shook his head in the passenger's seat of Jerry's Lincoln minivan.

"Fools," Jeff muttered.

Both men were competitive. Jeff, a large, tall, handsome man, wasn't used to losing. His size alone commanded respect and had made him a competitor at recess in school. Combined with his intellect, he was an asset to any team. Just tell him the objective, then get out of the way and let him figure out the best way to achieve it. He wasn't used to losing and he viciously hated it whenever he did lose. According to his calculations, losing wasn't probable and never should have happened.

Jerry, on the other hand, was never the best on his team, but only because he was smart enough to pick the best players on the playground. He was always clear about who he thought was good enough to be on his team and likewise was always brutally clear about who he felt didn't belong on his team. He surrounded himself with the best people and that made it easy to convince himself that he was better than he actually was. For him, losing was everyone else's fault. "You big dumb idiot! What kind of play was that?"

As his children grew up and became more demanding, the pressure on Jerry to not fail was building up. He already was one of the top salespeople in the region at Simbiox. But his family wanted to go to Disney and he needed a new car. He was sick of driving around his stupid minivan. His friends had sports cars. And his father-in-law had been looking at him critically lately, asking Jerry why he hadn't moved up higher in the company. "I thought he'd be an executive by now," Jerry once overheard his father-in-law saying.

Top in the region was great, but this year there was a bonus for the top sales team in the country, and after Jerry shared the numbers with Jeff, it was clear that if they put in the work, they could compete nationally. Number one was in their sights, but they needed the 100% participation bonuses that would come with enrolling 100% of employees at a business in the retirement plan.

When Vanessa's body turned up and Coffee Bucket sprang to 100% participation in the retirement plan, Jerry recalled Jeff's phone call.

"Let's not talk about it," Jerry said to Jeff.

Jerry had always thought something was off with Jeff. But did he murder Vanessa just so they could jump in the numbers? The rankings were online and Jerry took a peak that night. They had risen to the top 15 in the nation. This was huge.

"You know, that guy at Chevrolait says he won't sign up for the plan," Jerry said casually in the van one day after picking up Jeff.

"What's worse is I spoke with another employee there and they told me they were hesitant to sign up because Jace wasn't planning on signing up," Jeff added. "He's a troublemaker. A ringleader."

"And a cocky little shit, to boot."

They were driving through the neighborhood near Chevrolait. Several houses had boarded up windows and many of the businesses were empty.

"It doesn't make sense. You'd think people would be smart enough to invest in their future. It explains why someone like Jace would live in a dump like this."

"Would be terrible if something happened to him."

The next day, while at Coffee Bucket, Jeff passed Jerry a piece of paper with three numbers on it. It was the combination of the lock on the closet that held the Coffee Bucket safe and Summer's recently acquired firearms.

"She signed her retirement papers while in the office. I saw her go into the closet and saw the guns. It wasn't hard for me to see her enter the combination--she didn't even try to hide it," Jeff explained to Jerry. "What can I say. I'm good with numbers."

Jeff took Summer to the bathroom to show her how the toilet wouldn't stop running.

"I think Detective Mills messed it up."

Jerry took the opportunity to sneak into the back room and snatch one of Summer's guns... and the silencer.

The plan was to apprehend Jace after work, like they had Vanessa. At Chevrolait the employees closed in pairs. Jeff would slash the tires on Jace's Corolla so that he'd be stuck there after his coworker had driven away. Then, he would shoot him.

"Make sure you steal his wallet this time," Jerry said, recalling how Jeff hadn't stolen any money from Coffee Bucket the night he murdered Vanessa, which ruled out armed robbery.

While Jeff was waiting for Jace's shift to end, Jerry would break into Jace's apartment to find the list of employees he and Vanessa had been working with.

"That way we'll know who to pressure into signing up for the plan,"

Jeff said. "And I have a feeling with Jace and Vanessa out of the picture, we shouldn't have any trouble getting the rest of the employees to fall in line. We'll have 100% signed up at every coffee shop in the city. And then we can start to work on hair salons and dog walking agencies."

The plan should have gone off without a hitch, but Jace didn't drive to work that day. The Corolla Jeff destroyed was Misty's. Misty's presence at Chevrolait had scared Jace away, causing him to leave work and head home early. While walking up the back porch he stumbled upon Jerry trying to break into his apartment.

While Jerry stood there unsuccessfully trying to explain himself to a freaked out Jace, Jeff arrived and shot Jace in the back right there on the porch. No one heard anything unusual and the next day Jeff and Jerry jumped to the top five on the national leaderboard.

According to their calculations, full participation at Coffee Bucket was all Jerry and Jeff needed to secure the number one position in the nation. The only person standing in their way was that lazy, idiot: Misty Cheevis.

She had gotten hired by Summer and was taking her good old time signing up for retirement. Offering excuse after excuse. Leaving work sick or drooling on the retirement forms as she drifted off to sleep while Jerry tried to explain the plan to her. Misty alone had caused their ranking to drop as they lost the 100% bonus at Coffee Bucket they thought they had secured with Vanessa's murder.

"This stuff's crazy. Did you know it kills AIDS?" Detective Mills held the bottle of Steramine tablets close to his face, reading the label.

Jeff and Jerry looked at each other and Jeff snagged a bottle of the little blue tablets the next time he saw an opportunity.

A few days later, the opportunity presented itself.

Misty was tired and wanted a coffee for herself before heading to the Aquaponics warehouse. Jerry and Jeff had just finished signing Mr. Larry up for retirement. While they were doing so, Jeff slipped outside and left a note on Misty's bicycle.

"Leave town or you're next. Sincerely, The Cleveland Coffee Killer."

After he signed his papers, Mr. Larry offered to prepare a cup of coffee for Misty. It wasn't hard for Jeff to slip several of the tablets into the coffee under the old man's nose before he stirred in Misty's cream and sugar.

Jeff and Jerry were satisfied watching her take a huge sip. To Misty, coffee always tasted bad--that's why she loaded it with extras. Her face didn't register any difference in taste as Jeff and Jerry watched her take another gulp.

"I put enough Steramine in your coffee to kill a small cow," Jeff said, stepping into the light from behind the Super Coffee Coffee Drive-Thru dumpster.

It was cold and dark and Misty stood there in her stupid Super Coffee Coffee Drive-Thru uniform. She let the bag of trash drop onto the cracked asphalt as Jerry stepped into the light.

"What made you think we were dealing with a small cow, Jeff?" he added, with a chuckle.

"You killed Vanessa," Misty said. "And Jace! Why? Why would you do that? Why you?"

"Oh," Jeff said. "You wouldn't understand. It requires logic to understand our motivation. We're looking for results, something you're not familiar with. You should have just signed up for the retirement plan, Misty. It's so easy. It's free money."

"All you had to do was sign up, Misty, and this would have been much easier, much more efficient. We were so close. We are so close. Number one and the bonus are nearly in our hands! I have a family, Misty. I have kids to feed. A wife to please. A lonely dyke like you wouldn't understand the kind of pressure I'm under!"

"I did sign up!" Misty said.

"You signed the papers 'Tongue My Dumper,' Misty," Jerry responded.

"You guys actually check the signature?"

"Of course we check the signature!" Jeff was fuming. "Why would we have you sign all those papers if it didn't mean anything? What is wrong with you people?" Jeff slammed his fist against the side of the dumpster, the loud metal bang echoing through the empty parking lot.

"I didn't think it was a big deal!" Misty whined.

"We usually don't even check, but you initialed everything with TMD, so we checked your signature to see if maybe you had a different legal name than Misty Cheevis, but nope, you signed Tongue My Dumper and initialed it TMD." Jerry was grinning like a mad man and huffing and puffing in exasperation. He was mortified and amused by Misty's behavior. "So, no, you're actually NOT signed up for the retirement plan. And neither is Mr. Larry! He's supposed to be here!"

"I called him an Uber," Misty said. "I guess you'll just have to kill me tonight. So, how are you going to do it? The old boxcutter method? Did you steal another one of Summer's guns? Steramine obviously isn't lethal on me. So what's it gonna be?"

Misty could hear the sound of cars streaming by on the interstate highway just below Super Coffee. She knew that the sound would drown out even her loudest screams. She just had to stall as best she could.

"Well," Jeff said. "I thought we could inject you with Steramine. Make it look like you had a Steramine addiction or something. Like on one of those TV shows, where poor, ugly people share their strange addictions to eating couches or pennies or whatever. It wouldn't take much imagination to believe a freak like you was addicted to sanitizing tablets."

"And I thought we should just hit you over the head with a cinder block," Jerry argued. "Simple. Effective. Cinder blocks aren't hard to find. It would be efficient. Oh, look. There's one right here!"

Jerry picked up a cinder block from behind the dumpster.

"But it would lack style and taste," Jeff said. "It's just so vulgar and pedestrian."

"Well, we could strangle her with a Prada handbag, Jeff. Would you prefer that?"

Jeff got a look in his eye. "A trash bag."

"What?" Jerry said.

"It's sleek. Black. Shiny. And if we wrap it around her head... she won't be able to breathe."

"I love it," Jerry agreed. He then lifted up the large cinder block. "I think I'll just crack her over the head first. It'll be easier to slip the bag around her head if she's unconscious."

Misty felt a lump in her throat. She took a step back, preparing to launch herself at her enemies.

"I'm gonna fuck you up," she said, out loud. "I'm gonna fuck you up good."

Suddenly two headlights flashed on. The sound of AC/DC blared from the speakers.

The car screeched to a halt and the door of the golden Toyota Celica flew open. Gus stepped out, wearing a wife beater, jean shorts, knee socks and combat boots. He held a baseball bat in his hand.

"We looking for a brawl?" he asked, his headlights blinding Jeff and Jerry as they backed up against the dumpster. "Might as well make it a fair fight."

"What?" Jerry cried. "What's going on?"

"We got your ass," Misty said. "That's what's up."

"You can't! I have a family!"

"Then they can visit your ass in jail," Misty said. "Where you're gonna get raped!"

"Whoa. Jesus, Misty," Gus said, looking at Misty with distaste.

"What? I'm amped up!"

A flash of light glimmered from Jeff's hand. The tall, handsome man had released a knife from up his sleeve. He lunged at Misty. Gus ran toward him but as he did, Jerry swung the cinder block directly into his stomach, knocking the wind from his lungs.

Misty dodged Jeff's first lunge, grabbing his arm and swinging him forward, propelling him into the ground.

Misty's scream was muffled by the sound of cars speeding along the highway down below.

Jerry picked up Gus's bat and looked at Misty, who was kneeling on the ground near Gus.

He ran toward Misty with the bat raised above his head. Rage took over Misty's body and she launched herself at Jerry, spearing him like a professional wrestler. He went down hard and his head smacked into the newly poured drive-thru asphalt.

Jeff rose from the ground as Misty recovered. He had a huge crazy smile on his face. Like a real crazy person. He was foaming from the mouth. He held the blade in his hands and crept forward. He was huge and strong and wearing khakis and a button down.

Misty struggled to get up from the ground. She'd hurt her knee--an injury she'd had since a kickball accident in fourth grade. Never been the same since. He started to creep a little faster toward Misty.

Seeing Jeff lurking toward his girl, Gus rolled over on his side to lift himself up, but Jeff saw and kicked him hard in the face, knocking him back to the asphalt.

"Misty!" Gus croaked.

But Misty didn't hear it. Her ears were still ringing from the fall she'd taken.

Jeff prepared himself for the attack. Pulling his knife back and speeding up to rush toward Misty.

"SMASH!"

The 1988 Toyota Celica smashed into Jeff, pinning him against the side of the Super Coffee building. His body fell limp.

The driver's side door opened up and Tramaine came out. She was wearing her torn jeans, a hoodie and a pair of large headphones around her neck.

"Sorry. I don't drive. Took me a second to figure out how to get the thing out of park."

Misty collapsed to the ground, exhausted.

EPILOGUE

-

WELL I GUESS I BROKE PAROLE OR SOMETHING for almost killing two men. My lawyer says we'll be able to prove it was self defense in court. I had called Tramaine from Super Coffee that night and told her and Gus to come help me. She came through the drive through and handed me one of her highly sensitive ASMR microphones. We recorded Jeff and Jerry's entire confession that night. So Janice says I should get off fine, but I still have to attend more court-ordered therapy lessons with Janice. That means more gay ass journal entries. Barf. I know you're reading this, Janice--don't even fuck with me right now.

Also, it wasn't a cab that picked up Mr. Larry. It was Gus. Once I found out I was poisoned with Steramine, I knew it had to be someone who had given me food or something to drink that day--it narrowed down the field of suspects. At first I thought it was Mr. Larry, since he gave me that coffee, which in retrospect did taste funky. But then I remembered who was sitting there with Mr. Larry when he made up my drink. When Mr. Larry told me he hadn't signed the retirement plan yet, I heard alarm bells. I called Gus and Tramaine and told them to come get Mr. Larry out of here as fast as they could and then come back and drive my stupid ass home. Well, they didn't make it back before Jeff and Jerry confronted me, but I was able to stall until they got there. Who says talking shit doesn't get you anywhere?

What really pisses me off is that the police have taken full credit for this catch as if they didn't arrest and cavity search Summer weeks ago. Assholes. I saw Detective Poopy Pants giving a press conference in front of the Justice Center: wearing a shit-eating grin and bragging about apprehending the killers as if he had anything to do with it. INCORRECT. He didn't do shit except arrest an innocent barista who likes to play dress-up and pretend she's a cowboy. What a dumbass.

Summer's out of jail, though. I'm happy for her. She's back at her apartment. She visits me here and shows me pictures of the fish. Those things are spoiled as fuck but whatever makes Summer happy I guess. Grandma came back to Cleveland from Florida. I guess there was a chlamydia outbreak in the retirement community that was traced back to the guy she was seeing. So she moved back and said I could live with her, but I decided to keep my spot with Tramaine at the sober house.

Oh, and I might have a job after I get out. As it turns out, Vanessa didn't even steal the Aquaman Vegetable Wall blueprints. Big Ben stole them. Dick Vagantis had them hire Big Ben pretending it was about compost, but he was actually there to steal the plant wall technology to use in his weed business.

I figured out it was Big Ben and not Vanessa when I realized he was responsible for that musky odor that I'd gagged over when I got kidnapped. I thought it was the plant wall, but when Big Ben left the conference room and I could smell Michelle's fancy ass perfume, I knew the smell was his. That meant he was in the van and at the mattress factory with me when I got kidnapped. Busted. They fired his ass and they said they wanted to offer me a job. If the job is shoveling shit like Big Ben did, I think I might be good at it.

Oh yeah, and the Aquatopics guys also threatened to sue Dick Vagantis. Michelle has those connections--don't mess with that bitch. She's official. High profile. Yeah, so Vagantis didn't want to deal with any of that legal shit so he forgave the Aquaponics company of their debts. They also made him agree to leave me alone, which is a relief because even though Gus offered to show me how to counter nunchucks using just a ballpoint pen, I'd still rather avoid being attacked by someone swinging those things around.

Oh yeah, and before I got arrested I got to watch Gus crying over his wrecked Celica. Hilarious. He had tears streaming down his face. What a baby.

Tramaine felt so bad. She kept telling him she was sorry and that she did it to save my life, but Gus didn't want to hear it. He was like, "Yeah. Yeah. I need some alone time." What a little bitch.

I told him he just cared more about his car than he cares about me because his car flashes him its headlights more than I do and then as I was being arrested I flashed him my tits. HAHAHA! It was so hot. I could tell he wanted my ass and honestly I've been all horned up ever since. I can't wait to get out of here so we can fuck.

God. I'm like a wet mop down there just thinking about it.

All right. Janice told me I had to write a whole page and I think I did it, so I'm done.

Peace out, bitches! Misty <3

ABOUT THE AUTHOR

Kellen Alexander is a writer and barista.
They live in Cleveland, Ohio with their cat, Pez.
@kellenauthor
(Don't forget to leave a review! xoxo)